young inventor

Don't Miss Tom's Next Adventures!

TOM SWIFT™
young inventor

#5 ON TOP OF THE WORLD

By Victor Appleton

Aladdin Paperbacks
New York London Toronto Sydney

This book is a work of fiction. Any references to historical events,
real people, or real locales are used fictitiously. Other names,
characters, places, and incidents are the product of the author's
imagination, and any resemblance to actual events or locales or
persons, living or dead, is entirely coincidental.

ALADDIN PAPERBACKS
An imprint of Simon & Schuster Children's Publishing Division
1230 Avenue of the Americas, New York, NY 10020
Copyright © 2007 S&S Inc.

Designed by Lisa Vega
The text of this book was set in Weiss.
Manufactured in the United States of America
First Aladdin Paperbacks edition May 2007
2 4 6 8 10 9 7 5 3 1

Library of Congress Control Number 2007923949
ISBN-13: 978-1-4169-3643-5
ISBN-10: 1-4169-3643-2

Contents

ON TOP OF THE WORLD

Foiled Plans

"Yeah, baby!" I shouted as my snowboard carved around a stand of Scotch pines.

I glanced back to see Yolanda Aponte slice through a mogul of fresh powder, her skis kicking up a majestic rooster tail of snow. Farther back— *much* farther back—Bud Barclay crouched unsteadily over his gleaming red snowboard as he hit the same patch. Miraculously Bud managed to bounce through upright.

"Dude!" he yelled down at me. "No fair! We can't keep up!"

"Really?" I shouted back.

I leaned hard and cut a sharp crescent in the soft, glittering swale, veering my board uphill. Then I really began to pick up speed.

Yes, you read right. I turned uphill . . . *and started going faster*.

"Cheater!" called Yo, laughing and carving to a sudden halt.

Bud screeched to a hockey-style stop next to Yo, whipped out his mini digital video camera, and trained it on me.

"Kids will freak when they see the digital captures I pull from *this* footage," he called. "Dude, every snowboarder in Shopton will want a copy of next week's *Sentinel*."

Bud Barclay, my best friend since first grade, was the senior reporter for our high school newspaper, the Shopton Sentinel. He got a lot of journalistic mileage out of my inventions, which often led us to adventures in sometimes unusual places.

Suddenly my board clacked over an exposed rock, popping up hard. When I landed I caught an edge. I flopped face-first and did a brutal face-plant— the kind many a normal off-trail snowboarder has suffered up here in the wild Mount Shopton backcountry.

Of course I wasn't your normal off-trail snowboarder.

Halfway into the flop I gave a quick yank on a control bar slung horizontally in front of me. Then, howling like an insane wolf, I lifted vertically. My legs kicked up, whipping my superlight board back under me in a graceful arc.

Just for fun, I pulled back harder on the bar.

This took me airborne over another jagged outcropping of rock. I kept pulling on the bar; I pitched straight up and felt my feet arc forward, then flip over my head. For a second the flip disoriented me, but I trusted my equipment and my instinct; I'd practiced this move many times. As I completed a full reverse 360-degree loop, the board touched down gently—yes, my friends, on the *upslope* side of the big boulder.

"Pure sweetness!" shouted Bud in delight, filming the whole maneuver.

"Nice!" called Yo.

She put thumb and forefinger to her mouth and blasted a whistle that no doubt triggered wildlife stampedes and avalanches for miles around. I admit it; I'm jealous. I've tried for years to imitate Yo's whistle, but the best I can do is a pathetic, spitting noise that sounds like someone letting the air out of wet balloon.

So instead of returning the whistle, I rose thirty feet straight up in the air.

Okay, readers—maybe I've kept you in suspense long enough.

No, I'm not superhuman. (Not yet anyway; I'm working on some pretty cool cybernetic devices that might help.) The horizontal bar I mentioned was the control bar of an ultralight foil kite that I'd been working on for nearly a year.

Maybe you've heard of snow-kiting; it's been around awhile. But not quite like this. First, my kite was constructed of Swift-Foil, a revolutionary, light but rugged material that by itself would make the kite merely amazing. Second, with help from Yo and Ranjeet Patel, director of the Swift Enterprises computer lab, I'd also designed kite lines and a harness managed by a computerized avionics control bar. Just a twitch of the wrist could adjust the sail's trim, letting me change speed and trajectory with remarkably accurate control. In fact my stunt loop was so easy I felt almost embarrassed at all the cheering and whistling.

"How'd the board hold up?" called Yo.

"Tough as nails!" I yelled back.

This trek also featured the debut of a new snowboard I'd designed: the SwiftBoard, light as a molded foam beach board but tougher than any snowboard you've ever seen. I'd made it superlight by injecting silicon oxide crystals instead of ordinary resin into the microscopic voids between the fibers.

I know, I know—you're probably going, "Why didn't I think of that?" I agree—it *is* pretty elementary. Hey, sometimes being a world-class inventor means just seeing the obvious. Anybody who knows the properties of silicon oxide might have done the same.

Anyway, I'd been down this wild western slope of Mount Shopton many times since Dad first brought me up here when I was ten. Casmir Trent, Dad's bodyguard, would pilot the Swift Enterprises hovercraft, the SE-15, just under the summit and drop us above the tree line onto High Sentry Swale. *Whooosh!* Downhill we'd go, following a switchback course well known to backcountry skiers and boarders around here.

Over the years, Bud and Yo have been up here with me many times as well. But now here I was, hopscotching up and down the slope in a whole new way.

Bud and Yo waited as I caught a stiff upslope breeze, banked the kite around, and floated in place like a hawk riding a thermal. Then I pitched down to a gentle landing next to them. With a quick clockwise twist of the control bar, I activated a mechanism that folded up the kite.

Now I could stand next to Bud and Yo without getting blown away by a sudden gust.

"Looks like you've got a pretty feathery control touch there," said Yo.

"It's perfect," I said. "Sister, your fine-tuning is right on the money."

"Of course it is," said Yo, creasing her eyebrows. "I wasn't worried about the avionics." She shot me a dry look. "I'm more concerned about pilot error."

"Gee, thanks," I said.

"Hey," she said. "It's not like you've never made an impulsive decision."

Bud cleared his throat. He swiveled his minicam toward Yo.

"Question here!" he called out with the tone of a muckraking reporter rooting out scandal. "Are you suggesting that Tom Swift takes chances best described as rash, perhaps even . . . reckless?"

"Yes," answered Yo. "Yes, that's exactly what I'm suggesting."

"Interesting allegations," murmured Bud quietly.

"Plus he's ugly," said Yo, giving me an amused look.

Bud nodded. "Yes, my investigation has led me to that conclusion, but I'll need confirmation on that from a second source."

I grinned. "I'll confirm that," I said, raising my hand. "I'm ugly."

"Excellent!" exclaimed Bud. He nodded and flicked off the minicam. "This story should blow the cover off the whole Tom Swift myth."

Suddenly a series of beeps sounded from my wrist. I pulled back my ski jacket sleeve to reveal my minicom watch. The watch started coughing.

"Can I get some air here?" asked the watch in a choked voice.

We all looked at it for a second. It kept coughing.

"You okay there?" I asked the watch.

"Negative," said the watch, now speaking in a

hollow robotic voice. "Warning. Boot sector error. System reboot imminent."

I rolled my eyes. "Come on, Q.U.I.P.," I said. "Knock it off."

"I'm preparing to fire the missiles now, Dave," said the watch calmly, now sounding like HAL, the computer in 2001: *A Space Odyssey*.

Bud and Yo started laughing.

"Thank you," said the watch in the voice of a normal male teen. "Thank you very much."

I stared down at my watch . . . which of course was the current residence of the artificial intelligence entity known as Q.U.I.P., an acronym for Quantum Utilizing Interactive Processor.

"Don't look at me like that," said Q.U.I.P.

"Are you interrupting us for some good reason?" I asked.

"As a matter of fact, yes," replied Q.U.I.P. "I have a *very* good reason for interrupting your horseplay."

"Horseplay?" I repeated. "This is no horseplay. I have a serious purpose in testing this equipment today, as you well know."

Q.U.I.P. hissed at me in a loud stage whisper. "Yes, *I* know, but . . . do *they* know?"

I glanced over at Bud and Yo. I said, "Uh, I told you guys about Mount Everest, right?"

Yo and Bud exchanged a look.

"No, Tom," replied Bud. "I don't believe you told us about Mount Everest."

I smiled. "Well, I thought maybe we'd take the Swift Sub-Orbiter to Nepal on Monday," I said. "You know . . . for the holidays." I turned to Yo. "So we can test out that new climber-bot we've been working on."

Bud's eyes grew extremely large.

"Nepal!" he exclaimed.

Yo, on the other hand, narrowed her eyes. "Tom Swift, you *rat*," she groaned. "You *would* pick next week, wouldn't you?"

"What's wrong with next week?" I asked. I'd picked the holiday week so that none of us would have to miss any school. "It's perfect. I thought we could give our prototype a real test at altitude, you know, up on the Khumbu Icefall."

"What's an icefall?" asked Bud.

Q.U.I.P. reverted to his goofy 1950s robotic voice again. "Icefall," he droned. "Steep, treacherous glacial ice field characterized by rapid downward flow, crumbling ice towers called seracs, and lethal hidden crevasses. *Beep!* Danger! Danger! Danger!"

I clamped my hand over Q.U.I.P. "There's an icefall at the head of Khumbu Glacier under the southwest face of Mount Everest," I said.

Q.U.I.P. beeped again. We could hear his muffled voice under my hand: "Very risky. *Beep.* Very perilous."

Yo looked at Q.U.I.P., then at me, with forlorn eyes. "I can't go," she said.

"What?" I said loudly. "Why not?"

"Big family reunion," she sighed. "Planned for, like, years. Apontes from all over, including aunts and uncles from Puerto Rico I've never met." She shook her head. "No way can I miss it."

"Sneak out!" suggested Bud.

Yo gave him a look. "They'd find me," she said.

"In Nepal?"

"You know my mother," said Yo.

Bud nodded. "You're right," he said. "She'd find you in Nepal."

Yolanda Aponte has a very dry sense of humor, and she can be pretty sarcastic sometimes. But not even ski goggles could hide the look of disappointment in her eyes, and I felt pretty bad. Along with Bud, Yo's about as good a friend as a guy could have. Plus she had a real stake in the new robot I planned to test out. Yo helped design the software for its computer modules.

Suddenly Q.U.I.P. started honking, like a National Weather Service hazardous weather alert.

"What now?" I said, holding up my wrist.

"The reason for my interruption," said Q.U.I.P. "Remember?"

"Okay," I said. "So what's up?"

"Winter storm warning," said Q.U.I.P. "High winds, heavy snowfall, eight to twelve inches, blowing and drifting snow likely. Expect blizzard and whiteout conditions in the high country." Q.U.I.P. cleared his voice. "Which, by the way, is where we happen to be right now."

I nodded. "Okay, let's get out of here," I said.

Yo stabbed her ski poles into the ground and lifted off the rock cleft where she'd been standing. Crouching into a full Alpine tuck position, skis parallel, she began schussing straight down the fall line of the mountain.

"See you two dog-meat boarders down in

South Meadow," she yelled back. (Yo's just a little competitive.) "I'm sure I won't see you before then, since you'll be so . . . *far* . . . *behind me.*"

"Q.U.I.P., contact Casmir Trent," I said, quickly wrapping a Velcro strap around the folded kite. "Tell him we'll be waiting for the SE-15 at South Meadow in about ten minutes." I grinned and kicked my front foot downhill. "Actually make that *seven* minutes."

Next to me Bud groaned.

"Come on, dude!" I called. "Let's get down this bunny slope."

"Great," said Bud nervously. "Go ahead. I'll be . . . right behind you."

With a maniacal hoot, I sped down after Yo.

2

An Abominable Journey

Cruising at Mach 6 more than 120 kilometers above the Earth's surface creates some interesting effects in a flight cabin.

For example, as I gazed out the pilot-side window at the dark blue splendor of the Atlantic Ocean below, I felt something nudge the back of my head. I reached up to brush away what felt like an insect . . . and then jumped when I felt a much larger rectangular object.

I turned to see Bud's MP3 player floating in front of my face.

"Uh, Bud," I said, glancing over at him. He sat in the copilot's chair, gazing raptly out at the view.

"Yeah," he answered.

"Your tunes, dude," I said. I reached up and gave the player a tap; it floated toward Bud.

Bud turned toward me, then did a double take. "Whoa!" he said, plucking the MP3 player out of the air.

In a typical sub-orbital flight, you generally experience about five to seven minutes of continuous weightlessness. This happens at apogee, the highest point in the flight trajectory. I'd told Bud to prepare for it, but . . . well, it's not something you ever really get used to.

I started laughing. I pointed at Bud's head.

"Your hair," I said. "Awesome!"

Bud's floppy shock of hair was billowing around his head. He unbuckled his seat belt and rose out of his chair—literally. Straight up. Using the chair's armrests, Bud flipped himself around and pushed off toward the rear of the flight cabin.

"This totally rocks!" he said.

Bud glided to the restroom door, pulled it open, and looked at himself in the mirror inside. Then he started hooting like a deranged owl at the sight of his undulating hair.

"I wish it would do that all the time," he said, grinning out at me. "Especially at dances."

A gentle tone sounded from the flight control panel in front of me.

I said, "Yes, Q.U.I.P.?"

"The captain has asked me to inform you that we've crossed into another time zone," said Q.U.I.P. in the pleasant voice of a flight attendant.

"Thanks, Q.U.I.P.," I replied. "But I believe *I'm* the captain."

"So?" said Q.U.I.P. defensively. "Anyway, I've adjusted all clocks accordingly."

"Well done," I said. "You're a good servant."

"If you ever call me that again, I'm taking this craft straight down," said Q.U.I.P. "I control the autopilot, you know."

"Yes, I know," I said, trying not to laugh. "And please put Nepal on the interactive in-flight screen, will you?"

"Yes, master," replied Q.U.I.P.

Bud floated back to his copilot's seat and buckled himself in. "This is something everyone should experience at least once," he said.

"How do you feel?" I asked.

"Giddy with insane happiness," he answered.

"I told you," I said, grinning.

"But, dude, I'm glad you told me to eat light before we left," he added. He patted his stomach.

"Yes, lack of gravity can do funny things to your lunch," I said.

Another tone sounded, and a large flat-panel display flickered to life just below the Sub-Orbiter's instrument panel. The screen showed a world map with a red line running east from Shopton in upstate New York. It headed across the Atlantic Ocean then veered slightly south over the Mediterranean Sea, finally curving down across the Middle East into southern Asia.

"Is that our course?" asked Bud.

"You got it," I answered. I pointed at a yellow blip just over Spain. "That's us."

"Holy cow," said Bud.

At hypersonic speed, time feels different, even though it isn't really. Flying Mach 6 at an altitude of roughly 250,000 feet, you're traveling about 3600 mph. The distance from Shopton, New York, to our refueling destination of Lukla, Nepal, was approximately 7500 miles. Do the math. Okay, okay . . . I'll do that math. That translates to a travel time of just over two hours.

Incredible, eh?

Two hours of flight time, and suddenly you're dropping onto the planet's rooftop known as the Himalayas. That's just sick.

"Q.U.I.P., please give us Everest, south side," I said.

"Roger that," said Q.U.I.P.

The country of Nepal grew to full size on the display screen. Then the map zoomed into the region just south of Mount Everest, which sits on the northern border of Nepal. Onscreen, the mountainous terrain slowly rose in three-dimensional splendor as the zoom-in progressed. Our satellite-linked Swift Geo-Mapping Project software updated the planetary surface in full 3-D every thirty minutes, so I knew we were looking at a fresh image.

"Now zoom the South Col route," I said.

"Aye, aye, sir," said Q.U.I.P.

"And bring up that other stuff you found," I added. I glanced over at Bud. "Dude, you might want to get out your notebook."

Bud opened a small compartment next to his seat and eagerly whipped out his news reporter's pad and pen.

"Ready," he said.

The map zoomed in on the great white peak from above, and then swiveled in an arc to a side view of the mountain. Now we were looking at Everest's famous south face. Six blue dots popped onscreen up the side of the slope, each labeled by name and altitude: Base Camp (17,500 feet) at the bottom, then Camp I (19,500 feet), and so on up to Summit (29,028 feet) . . . a spot that sits, literally, at the top of the world.

"So we're looking at the most popular route up Mount Everest, the one taken by Sir Edmund Hillary and Tenzing Norgay on the first-ever ascent to the summit," I said. "Most climbers who take a shot at Everest use this route, and start right here." I pointed at the blue dot labeled "Base Camp." "That's where we're headed. It sits just below the massive Khumbu Glacier."

Bud squinted at the screen. "Tom, does that say 17,500 feet?" he asked.

"Yep," I said.

"So, even at Base Camp . . . aren't we pretty darned *high up?*" asked Bud.

"Yes, we are," I answered, nodding. "Very, very high up."

"Like, about three miles higher than Shopton?"

"Correct."

"So . . . won't altitude sickness be a serious problem for us?" he asked.

"Normally, yes," I answered. "But this Sub-Orbiter's flight deck is also a graduated pressure compartment." I gestured around the cabin. "As we sit here, the air pressure and oxygen levels are dropping, little by little. You won't even notice the changes, but the adjustments are designed to help our bodies acclimate to the altitude at Base Camp."

Bud shook his head and started jotting notes.

"This craft is amazing," he murmured. "I suppose it serves hot cocoa, too."

Ding! A small microwave compartment door popped open next to the display screen. A tray emerged with a steaming mug of hot cocoa.

Bud stared down at it. "Somebody's a wise guy."

"Q.U.I.P., bring up those cryptid files, will you?" I asked.

"Your wish . . . is my command, sahib," replied Q.U.I.P.

Several onscreen windows popped open down the left side of the display screen.

"Cryptid?" asked Bud. "What the heck is a cryptid?"

One of the windows displayed a page with the title "Cryptozoology." I reached out and touched the window, and it zoomed to full size. Icons of several strange creatures were arrayed beneath it. I reached out and touched an icon labeled "The Kraken." An 1801 drawing by a French artist appeared full-screen, showing a giant squidlike creature pulling down the masts of a French sailing vessel.

"'Cryptid' is a term for any mystery creature said to exist but never officially *proven* to exist," I explained. "An obvious example would be the Loch Ness Monster in Scotland. Everybody's heard of that." Then I pointed at the display screen. "Another is the kraken here. French sailors described being attacked by such a creature off the coast of Angola."

"That's frightening," said Bud. He grinned and touched his billowing, weightless hair. "It makes my hair stand on end."

This cracked me up. Hey, Bud's a funny guy.

"Well, in the case of the kraken," I said, "it turns out maybe those sailors weren't just hallucinating." I touched the kraken drawing and a new window popped up: a murky photograph of huge tentacles draped across the screen. "As we now know," I continued, "the giant squid is an actual, living sea creature that can grow up to *at least* fifty feet in length, and maybe even bigger."

"I've seen that shot before," said Bud.

"Yeah, it's pretty famous," I said. "A team of Japanese scientists snapped this first-ever photo of a giant squid just a few years ago. This ugly beast attacked some bait they'd dropped to a depth of three thousand feet. The squid got snagged in the lure, and finally broke free." I gave Bud a look. "It left behind a torn tentacle almost *eighteen feet long*."

"Terrifying," said Bud, nodding. "But why do we care? Are there killer snow squids on Mount Everest?"

I laughed again. "No, but perhaps you've heard of *this* fellow," I said, tapping another onscreen icon.

The icon zoomed big, showing a grainy frame of video. In it, a tall, apelike creature was frozen in midstride along the sandbar of a creek. I tapped the screen again to trigger the video. The creature lumbered off into the tree line.

"Bigfoot!" exclaimed Bud.

"Bingo," I said. "This is the famous 1967 film shot by some guy up in northern California."

"Wasn't that a hoax?" asked Bud.

"Most people think so," I said. "But nobody can prove it one way or the other."

I touched the bigfoot video window and it shrunk down to icon size again. Then I tapped another icon. This one brought up a photo of a huge, shaggy, apelike creature towering over a normal-size man. A tag along the bottom read "*Gigantopithecus*: the Himalayan yeti?"

"Yikes!" said Bud, leaning back from the screen. "Is that real?"

"No, that's a statue," I said. "But it's a statue of a real primate—one that actually existed. The fossil record shows that *Gigantopithecus* roamed the Himalayas as recently as a hundred thousand years ago."

Bud eyed the onscreen tag. "'The Himalayan yeti,'" he read. Then he glanced warily at me. "The abominable snowman myth, right?"

"Right," I said. "But like the kraken, maybe there's something real behind the myth."

Outside, the space around the Sub-Orbiter began to brighten a bit. The sleek craft shuddered slightly and its nose pitched downward. We could see Earth's curved, greenish blue horizon creep up the glass of the forward windshield.

Then a voice crackled in the panel speakers.

"Uh, roger that, Houston," said Q.U.I.P. in the bland drawl of an old-school NASA flight controller. "We are full go, repeat, full go for atmospheric reentry at nineteen past apogee. All telemetry looks good. Contact with Ascension Island tracking station established. Rrrrrready to commence thermal conditioning roll."

Bud looked at me. "What is he talking about?" he asked.

"We're going down," I translated.

"Is that bad?"

"No, it's good."

"Well, then I'm happy," said Bud.

"We'll be rolling a few times to disperse thermal heat around the fuselage as we descend and brake to Mach three," I added, "so don't freak out when we flip upside down in a few seconds."

"Whatever," said Bud, waving his hands. "Can we get back to the topic at hand? I mean, what are you saying, man? That yetis actually exist?"

"Maybe," I said. "A lot of reputable scientists think it's entirely possible that an isolated tribe of protohumans could have survived the Ice Age up in the Himalayan high country."

"Protohumans?" repeated Bud.

"Dudes who are half-ape, half-man, walking upright and using tools," I said. "Map please, Q.U.I.P."

"I'm busy," answered Q.U.I.P.

"Doing what?" I asked.

"Thinking," said Q.U.I.P.

I smiled. "Can you multitask?"

"No, because I'm thinking about landing this five-ton craft."

"You can't give me a map of the Himalayas?" I said.

"Oh, all right."

A full 3-D topographical map of the Himalayas appeared onscreen. I swept my hand across the red-tinted mountain range.

"I mean, *look* at them," I said. "They're *huge*. Fifteen hundred miles long, two hundred miles deep. And a *lot* of that space is remote and inaccessible. It would be easy for a small band of cave dwellers to roam around undetected by humanity."

Bud gave me a skeptical look. Since we'd passed the high point of our sub-orbital flight path, the weightless effect was wearing off. Bud's hair was settling back to its normal look.

"You're suggesting that the abominable snowman might actually exist?" he asked.

I shrugged. "Check this out," I said, tapping one more onscreen icon.

Beep! A collage of pictures filled the screen: photos of gorillas, orangutans, and other apes next to shots of scientists holding up fossilized bones, skulls, and footprints, plus a few sketches of hominids based on fossil recreations.

"Here's the deal," I said. "Most cryptid sightings are based entirely on eyewitness accounts."

"Crackpots and kooks, mostly," said Bud.

"Yes," I agreed. "Mostly. But some very credible people have reported yeti sightings." I tapped a photo onscreen. "This is Eric Shipton, a mountaineering legend in England. He found huge, apelike footprints in the snow halfway up Everest in 1951."

"At 19,685 feet, to be exact," interjected Q.U.I.P.

"He took pictures," I said. "Very controversial pictures, yes, but nobody thinks Shipton is a fraud. And even Hillary and Norgay reported seeing large footprints on their historic First Summit in 1953." I leaned toward Bud, nodding emphatically. "These were not crackpots or kooks, my man."

"You're kidding, right?" said Bud.

"No," I said. "Plus yeti stories have some basis in actual zoology. Large hairy primates actually do exist today, Ever heard of gorillas? Orangutans?"

"Never," said Bud.

I ignored him and said, "Plus the South Asia fossil record contains several extinct primates that match the yeti's general description." I tapped the screen to bring up the big hairy ape statue again. "For example, *Gigantopithecus* here fits the description of the creature seen many times on Everest by local Sherpa tribesmen and a few Western climbers on expedition."

Bud stared at the screen. I could almost hear the news-reporter lobe of his brain buzzing and clicking. After a few seconds of thoughtful silence, he finally looked over at me. I could see a cautious but growing excitement in his eyes.

"What's the weather like in Nepal this time of year?" he asked.

"Abominable," I said.

He grinned. "Excellent," he said.

I felt the pull of gravity and noticed we'd rolled a full 180 degrees. Flying inverted, Bud and I could raise our heads and see the Asian subcontinent spread out in stunning swirls of color through the Sub-Orbiter's cockpit roof bubble.

Our descent to Nepal had begun.

Base Camp Blues

The airstrip at Lukla, Nepal, presents a harrowing test of flying skills. As the Sub-Orbiter popped out of the heavy cloud cover over Lamjura Pass, a rush of adrenaline flowed through me. Meanwhile my copilot gripped his armrests and looked ill.

"That's an *airport*?" gasped Bud.

"It's pretty small," I said.

"Tom, I think that's a parking lot."

"Trust me," I said.

Carved into the side of a mountain at an altitude of 9,380 feet, the Lukla airstrip is one of the highest in the world. The weather is very unpredictable. But even more unsettling is the runway's layout: a steep rock cliff rising at one end, and a sheer two-thousand-foot drop-off at the other end. Fun!

Thus, to land a typical aircraft in the town

known as the Gateway to the Himalayas, a pilot must perform a pretty hairy maneuver. Fortunately the Sub-Orbiter is no typical aircraft. The VTOL (Vertical Take Off and Landing) design is one of my dad's best, and I've gotten pretty good at the controls. Plus the autopilot remains active as a backup avionics system during landing, so I felt very secure dropping into the valley.

"Nice work," said Bud as we touched down gently on the tarmac.

"Thanks," I replied.

The Lukla refueling stop was prearranged by the Swift Enterprises travel service, so the airport crew was ready; Bud and I just sat in the cockpit as they worked. This was good, because we needed as much time as possible in the graduated pressure compartment. Most visitors to Everest spend eight days trekking from Lukla up to the Base Camp, resting in lodges along the way to get acclimated to the lofty altitude. Bud and I, on the other hand, were at sea level in Shopton just two hours earlier. And if everything went as planned, we'd be on the ground at Base Camp—over eight thousand feet *higher* than Lukla—in just forty-five minutes.

Bud watched an old villager lead a shaggy brown yak up a trail to the north.

"I think I'm getting cabin fever," he said.

"Why?" I asked.

"I'm seeing yaks," he said.

I laughed and checked the pressure readouts. The cabin now simulated an altitude of 14,000 feet. I could definitely feel the difference.

"I'm finding it harder to breathe," said Bud suddenly. He huffed a few deep breaths.

"Relax," I said. "You'll get used to it."

I wondered what it might be like to *double* this simulated altitude atop Everest. I knew that to reach the summit climbers pass through a moonscape plateau at 26,000 feet known as the Death Zone. There the sky darkens to an eerie blue as you trudge at the edge of outer space. At that height, the human body loses all ability to acclimate and begins to deteriorate. Biological functions like digestion begin to shut down from lack of oxygen. A bone-deep exhaustion sets in.

Bud eyed the old man and his animal again. "Do they run wild, these yaks?" he asked.

"I don't think so," I answered.

Bud nodded. "Because they're, like, really big," he said. He turned to look at me.

"Your eyes are kind of glazed there, dude," I said. "Maybe I'm depressurizing the cabin too quickly."

Bud nodded and said, "Tom, please don't let the yaks get me."

"I won't," I promised.

Grinning, I glanced over at the maintenance crew doing the refueling. One waved at me; I waved back. Beyond them, across the tarmac, a sleek, cobalt blue helicopter sat near a low metal shed. A name was painted in white on its tail boom: THE BLUE WASP. A man in a low-slung blue bush hat sat in the pilot's seat. He seemed to be staring at me.

"That's a nice bird," I said to Bud, nodding toward the copter.

Bud looked out my window. "'The Blue Wasp,'" he read. "What a name."

"It's one of those new Werewolf-class units with the modified coaxial rotor design," I said.

Bud gave me a blank look. "Speak English," he said.

I pointed at the helicopter. "See the two sets of rotors on top?"

"Yes."

"Those turn in opposite directions," I said. "That gives the craft much better stability, especially in high winds. Very good in the mountains. It's also very *quiet*. It was designed for military use in places like Afghanistan."

Two more men in bush hats stepped out of the shed carrying some equipment. Then a third man emerged with several long fabric cases slung over his shoulder. The men loaded their gear into the helicopter.

"What's in those long things, do you think?" asked Bud.

"Cross country skis, maybe," I suggested.

"Kind of *short* for skis," said Bud suspiciously. "Looks more like scoped rifle cases, if you ask me."

"Maybe they're yak hunters," I said.

Bud started chortling. "That's a good one, Swift," he said.

Refueling finished up smoothly, and in just thirty minutes we were airborne again.

I flew northeast, following the overland trek route used by most Everest expeditions. The white, double-humped upper reaches of the great mountain loomed ahead, clear and unclouded, so I drifted in for a closer look at the mountain's south side.

"Good gosh, that's awesome," said Bud in a hushed tone.

"Wow," was all I could say.

Everest, up close, in real life . . . *Dude!* Bud pointed out some of the famous stuff we'd read about the past few days. Near the bottom was the jagged icefall at the head of Khumbu Glacier. The glacier flows down through a bowl-like basin called the Western Cwm (pronounced "koom"); looming above that is the sheer, shiny ice wall called the Lhotse Face.

"There's the cornice ridge!" I said as I swung the Sub-Orbiter around the summit. We gazed down at a ridiculously narrow ridge that dropped sharply eight thousand feet on one side and ten thousand feet on the other.

Bud frowned with disbelief. "People *walk* on that?" he asked. "It looks like an ax blade."

"Exactly," I said. "Some climbers actually call it Knife Ridge."

Bud stared across at the distinctive black pyramid of the summit. A plume of ice crystals blew east from it. "I'm sure the view is sweet," he said. "But did you know the jet stream blows at hurricane force up there? It can drop temperatures to a hundred below zero." He shook his head. "Really, why would anybody climb onto that thing?"

"Because . . . *it's there*," intoned Q.U.I.P., echoing the famous words of mountaineer George Mallory.

Bud gave the control panel a look. "Whatever," he said.

I banked the Sub-Orbiter around the mountain one more time, and then made a tight little vertical landing just about a hundred yards from the Base Camp. As we touched down I noticed quite a few tents set up on the rocky slope below the glacier.

"Looks like we'll make some new friends," I said.

"Or enemies," said Bud.

I gave him a quick look. "Dude, mountaineers are good people," I said.

Bud gazed up at the majestic white peak rising above us, etched sharply on the blue sky.

"Okay," he said.

Two separate climbing teams were bivouacked at Base Camp, preparing to ascend Everest: one from

Australia and one from the United States. Two other groups were camped there too. But these were just hiking tours whose goal was simply to reach the famous camp, stay a day or two, and then return to Lukla.

Laughter echoed from a canvas pavilion tent about fifty yards uphill from the spot we'd chosen to make camp. Dusk was falling already. Smaller dome tents, glowing from lanterns inside, dotted the slope all around the bigger tent.

"Amazing," said Bud, shaking his head as he looked around. "Pretty crowded for such a lifeless little patch of rock."

I tried to answer but a coughing fit racked my raw throat.

"You sound great," said Bud.

I just shook my head miserably in response, still coughing. Bud grabbed his head and sat on a chunk of ice the size of a footstool. He winced in pain.

"You okay, man?" I finally managed to squawk.

"An invisible guy with an ice pick is stabbing me in the head," he said, massaging his temples.

Yes, the altitude was taking a toll on us. Bud's sharp headache had started almost the moment we descended from the cockpit. Within half an hour my throat felt like sandpaper. Apparently not even a slick, high-tech pressure chamber is a complete substitute for a gradual climb up to altitude.

Coughing again, I hammered in the last titanium stake to anchor the solar-powered SwiftCom Geo-Dome next to our two-man expedition tent. I adjusted its solar dish. Finally I ran a high-speed fiber-optic cable from the dome into our tent.

"What's this thing again?" asked Bud.

"It's a satellite link," I said. "Full communications access—Internet, cell phone, GPS receiver."

"Sweet," said Bud. "Can it pull in video games?"

I nodded. "Absolutely."

"Let me in."

"Okay, let's get inside," I said hoarsely.

We crawled into the tent. I'd already fired up the catalytic heater, so the place was toasty. I made sure the ventilation flap was open—even a flameless heater can produce deadly carbon monoxide gas. Then we unfolded a pair of camp chairs and a small table. Finally I set up a lantern with superbright LED bulbs.

"I think I'd better just sit here," said Bud, collapsing

heavily into his chair. "Like, for a couple of months."

I sat and nodded. "We'd better rest until morning at least," I said. "Then maybe we can hike up to the icefall and check it out."

More laughter drifted down the slope.

"We should probably introduce ourselves to some of the neighbors tomorrow, too," said Bud.

"Good plan," I replied. I plugged the fiber-optic cable into a slim, gel-screen PDA and tapped its power button. "Q.U.I.P., are you there?"

"Roger," said Q.U.I.P. from the PDA.

"Give me reports," I said.

"Weather good," replied Q.U.I.P. "Wind good." He made a chirping sound like R2-D2. "Basically, it's all good."

"Good," I said. I turned to Bud and held up the PDA. "Dude, you wanna check your e-mail or play a game or something?"

Bud tore open a Velcro pocket on the sleeve of his ski parka and pulled out a pack of playing cards.

"Actually, no," he said with a grin. "I'm thinking low-tech right now."

We played cards for hours. Hey, sometimes the simple things are the best.

Later, as we stuffed our weary bodies into our alpine "mummy-cut" sleeping bags, I heard the hissing blades of a helicopter hovering overhead for a few seconds. The tent ruffled in the downdraft; it must have been directly above us.

"Maybe it's those yak hunters," yawned Bud.

"Well, I'm *way* too tired to look," I said. Fatigue was really hitting me hard.

Soon all I could hear was the moan of wind on the mountain. As I drifted asleep, I listened to the distant crack and rumble of the vast ice sheet dropping slowly, inch by inch, down the side of Mount Everest.

Then, just for a second, I thought I heard a mournful howl.

4

Sherpa and Sherpbot

The next morning, Bud and I felt better—well, good enough to step outside the tent, anyway.

The weather was fine, and after cooking up a tasty breakfast of eggs and potatoes, we hiked down to the Sub-Orbiter to fetch my test subject: a robotic "Sherpa" named A.N.G.

The Sherpa, of course, are an ethnic group of Nepalese who live in the high Himalayas. But the term "Sherpa" also refers to native guides or porters (baggage-carriers) for mountaineering expeditions. Sherpas have amazing endurance and strength, and they know the mountains like you know your own house.

So A.N.G. was a "Sherpbot": a mechanical porter.

I unlatched the cargo hold and we slid out the large white crate.

"This is much lighter than it looks," said Bud with a grateful smile.

"Well, the crate itself is just injection-molded foam," I said. "But the robot is the cool thing. Most of the body is a magnesium alloy that's superlight and almost indestructible."

I popped open the crate and we lifted out a four-legged contraption about the size of a Saint Bernard. In fact, A.N.G. looked kind of doglike: four thick, hinged legs and a trunk for carrying heavy loads, plus a computer module "head" with video sensors and a laser scanner in its snout.

"'A.N.G.,'" read Bud. "What does that stand for?"

"Adaptive Neurotronic Gofer," I said, grinning. "He can carry two hundred pounds up a steep hill."

"I can see why you shortened that to A.N.G.," said Bud.

"Ang is a traditional Sherpa name," I said. "Ang Rita Sherpa is one of the most famous mountain climbers in the world. He's been to Everest's summit eleven times without supplemental oxygen."

"What?" exclaimed Bud. "That's sick!"

"I'll say," I said. "They call him the Snow Leopard."

Bud looked down at A.N.G. "Well, this guy is the Snow Dog."

"He's pretty cool, isn't he?" I said, nodding.

My watch suddenly beeped. Q.U.I.P.'s voice crackled from the microspeaker. "You like the dog better than you like me," said Q.U.I.P. gloomily.

I laughed. "Not yet," I said. "But it's certainly *possible*."

"Give me legs and an internal gyroscope and I could carry luggage up a hill too," sniffed Q.U.I.P.

"Actually I was thinking of doing just that," I said. "After we run some adaptability tests up on the icefall, I might download you into A.N.G.'s brain."

"Perfect!" blurted Bud. "Q.U.I.P. . . . *the dog brain*."

"Amusing, Mr. Barclay," said Q.U.I.P. "When I'm the dog brain and you see A.N.G. raise one of its hind legs"—he paused for effect—"I'd take cover if I were you."

I sighed. "Okay, knock it off, you two," I said. "Let's get going."

"Oh yes, let's," said Q.U.I.P.

I began to hike uphill. Frowning, Bud followed. "Are we leaving it here?" he asked.

"No," I said. When I reached the top of the rocky rise, I turned back toward the robot.

"A.N.G., *heel!*" I called out.

The mechanical pack animal began to trot at a fairly fast clip up the slope. The leg movement was so fluid and animal-like it was . . . well, almost creepy. Of course Yo and I had already done a lot of testing in the hills around Shopton. But I figured the Khumbu Glacier would be the acid test.

"Tom, he's heading right for that rock slide," said Bud, worried.

"I know," I said.

A.N.G. was moving straight toward a small boulder field, the remnants of an ancient avalanche. Bud and I had skirted around it as we traversed the hill. But A.N.G. just hopped onto the first rock and kept trotting. His foot placement was very accurate, but even if he slipped or rocks gave way under A.N.G.'s weight, he just kicked out feet on the opposite side for a very agile recovery.

"Awesome," said Bud.

"A.N.G., sit!" I called.

The robot obediently "crouched" with all of its joints hinged, looking now like a four-legged spider hunkering on a rock. I admired the mech-beast for a moment, then glanced over at Bud. He was rubbing one of his temples.

"Oh no," I said. "Headache again?"

"Not too bad," said Bud. "It kind of comes and goes."

"Maybe we should rest some more," I said with concern.

Bud waved off the suggestion. "Nah," he said. "Let's get this puppy up on the glacier."

"Puppy! Ha!" scoffed Q.U.I.P. from my wrist.

We led A.N.G. up the gentle slope to our campsite, where our hiking packs sat ready to go. I slung them both onto A.N.G.'s back, strapped them down, and set off toward the tent village in the heart of Base Camp. A.N.G. dutifully lumbered behind us.

"What a great way to meet the neighbors," said Bud, glancing back at the robot. "Does he do tricks, too?"

Needless to say, we drew a lot of attention. Hikers cooking, loading packs, or just sitting around jumped up and came running to see the odd mechanical creature. As I explained its function, a member of the Australian climbing team sidled up, laughing.

"Bonzer, mate!" he said. "A robot Sherpa. Brilliant!"

I smiled and patted A.N.G.

"Well, it's just a prototype, but—"

Whap!

A snowball exploded on the side of my head. Ringing with pain, I spun around to spot the thrower. I found myself looking into the angry glare of an exotic, dark-eyed teen girl.

"Is this how American boys treat their hosts?" she hissed.

"What?" I looked over at Bud, who just shrugged and slid behind one of the bigger Australian climbers. I turned back to the girl. "What are you talking about?"

"A robot Sherpa," she shouted. "Do you think this is amusing?"

"No," I said reflexively. I felt guilty of something, but I didn't know what.

Several stocky, dark-skinned men stepped up next to the girl. They didn't look too pleased either. It struck me that these were probably the Sherpa guides for the climbing teams. Some wore traditional suede Sherpa hats with sheepskin earflaps. But a few of the younger-looking guys wore baseball caps. One had a Yankees logo.

The girl was about to speak again, but an older Sherpa patted her arm then stepped forward.

"My name is Gombu," he said to me calmly.

"I'm Tom," I said. "Tom Swift."

I'm sure I looked pretty nervous, so he gave me a little smile and nod. Then he gestured back to the others behind him.

"We take people up the mountain," he said. "Guides, porters—this is what we do. It's what we've always done. It is our living." He spoke slowly, but quite clearly. "My father was a mountain guide. So was his father." He looked back toward the angry girl. "So is my daughter."

"Holy cow," I said. I pointed at A.N.G. "You think my robot will put you out of work?"

The girl stepped toward me. "Is that not its purpose?" she asked sharply.

"No!" I cried. "Not at all."

Several of the younger Sherpa men hovered behind her, looking . . . well, let's say *unhappy*. I felt unsteady enough from altitude sickness, but this unforeseen development got me pretty freaked out. But suddenly Bud moved up and stood shoulder to shoulder with me.

"Tom wouldn't do that!" said Bud. He was a little hot himself now. He looked at me, nodded, and said, "I got your back, bro."

This last phrase made me smile. I couldn't help it. It calmed me down, too. I turned to Gombu and said, "Let me explain, please."

Gombu bowed respectfully. Then he looked at me with calm eyes, waiting.

"No robot could *possibly* replace you," I said. "I've read a lot about your people and your amazing skills. Believe me, I call my robot here a Sherpa out of the deepest respect."

Gombu bowed again. But his daughter still looked unconvinced. I turned to face her.

"I see a future for robots like A.N.G. here, but not as Sherpas or even porters," I explained. "I see them going where no human can go—places like Mars or other planets. You could send them into combat or other risky rescue missions where it's too dangerous to send in human porters."

Yo and I had discussed these sorts of possibilities for hours while assembling and programming A.N.G.'s components, so I wasn't just blowing smoke here. I really believed that robots could play

46

valuable roles in hazardous situations like that. I think Gombu sensed my sincerity and how bad I felt, and he smiled. But his daughter still eyed me sort of suspiciously.

"Tom Swift, this is Pasang," said Gombu.

"Hello," I said with a sheepish smile.

Now Gombu gave his daughter a pointed look, then nodded toward me. She rolled her eyes, but then stepped toward me and extended her hand.

"Greetings," she said.

I shook her hand; her grip was strong. "You've got a nice arm," I said to her.

Puzzled, she looked down at her arm. I almost laughed, but said, "I mean, throwing." I mimicked a toss. "You nailed me good from at least twenty yards away." I rubbed the side of my jaw, which still ached from the snowball strike.

"Oh!" said Pasang. Some of the other Sherpas grinned at her now, then at me.

Two hours later we were all the best of friends.

"A.N.G., *slide!*" I called.

A.N.G., now bearing the weight of Gombu on its back, began scuttling sideways like a crab. Gombu was laughing with delight. Several of the older guides watched with great amusement.

I looked over at Bud, who was playing cards with Pasang and two teen Sherpa boys on our tent table, which we'd moved outside. He was teaching them a crazy game called Slapjack, and they were yelling and laughing as they played through rounds.

"I'm warning you," I called to them. "Bud cheats."

"No, no, no," called Pasang, smiling brightly. "We see everything. Cheating? Not possible."

"Don't listen to Tom," said Bud. "He's just sore because I beat him every time."

Earlier I'd learned that the Sherpa crews had two days of free time while the climbing teams recuperated from a tough training ascent. Yesterday, the guides had led the teams up to Camp III, near the top of the glacier at 23,700 feet, and then descended back to Base Camp; this was part of the acclimation plan. Now they planned to rest for forty-eight hours.

The Sherpa guides and porters, of course, needed no rest. They live up here. So when I learned they were available, I immediately hired both Gombu and Pasang to guide us up onto the Khumbu Icefall the next day. My dad had given me a travel budget that included money for this sort of thing.

"A.N.G., heel!" I called. Like a trusty dog, the robot hauled Gombu right to me. The man hopped off and bowed.

"That was most enjoyable," he said, beaming.

"Glad you enjoyed it," I said.

One of the other guides whispered something in Gombu's ear. He nodded and his face grew serious. I'd learned that Gombu was the sirdar, or leader of the team. The others clearly treated him with great respect.

"It is true," he said. "Tomorrow we make an expedition with you. Even though it is not long, we must prepare ourselves."

We said our good-byes. As Pasang nodded at me, she reached into a side pouch she was carrying and pulled out a sharp-looking white scarf. She presented it to me as a gift, explaining its traditional nature and offering with it a ritual blessing.

"Thanks," I said. "See you tomorrow."

"We hold a *puja* in the morning," she said. "You should join us."

"What's that?" I asked.

"A Buddhist ceremony asking the gods for permission to climb within their heights," said Pasang. "No Sherpa climbs Everest without a *puja*."

"We'll be there," I said.

"Very good, Tom Swift," she said.

"Hey, call me Tom, will you?" I asked.

"Very good, Tom."

And then the Sherpa team moved uphill to their campsite. Bud and I waved as they entered their tents, then took a last look at the mist-shrouded mountain looming over us.

5

Dancing on the Icefall

The next morning I awoke rested, happy, and eager to start trekking to the glacier. But when I heard the wretched moan coming from the next sleeping bag, I knew Bud wasn't sharing my state of mind.

"My head feels like a pineapple," he groaned.

I rolled over and looked at him. "Dude, I don't know what a pineapple feels like," I said. "But it can't be good."

"It's not," said Bud. "It's bad. Very bad." He rubbed his eyes. "I had insane dreams all night and woke up, like, eight hundred times."

We'd read up on acute mountain sickness (AMS), the medical name for altitude sickness. I knew that at 17,500 feet and above, where we would spend the next few days, the chance of suffering some form of AMS was pretty high. I also knew that if Bud's

symptoms were bad enough, I'd have to get him at least a thousand feet lower in order for him to recover and get properly acclimated.

"Tell me your symptoms," I said. I wanted to get him talking so I could gauge his brain function. If he seemed confused or disoriented, I knew I had a problem on my hands.

"Bad headache," he said. He sat up. "Whoa!" he said, and dropped back down. "Plus dizziness."

"Is that it?" I asked.

"Well, I feel an overwhelming urge to conjugate Latin verbs," he said.

I laughed. His sense of humor was intact. That was a good sign.

"I don't think this is severe or life-threatening," I said. "But obviously you're in no shape to hike." I unzipped my bag and slid out. "We can wait another day."

"No!" cried Bud. "Gombu and Pasang are only available today. You'll need their help across that icefall, man. Just go without me."

I looked at him carefully. His eyes looked normal. Then I heard footsteps crunching just outside the tent.

"Hello?" called a female voice.

"Pasang?" answered Bud.

I reached up and unzipped the tent flap. Two Black Diamond mountaineering mittens parted the flap, and Pasang leaned in. She wore a sky-blue stocking cap pulled low on her forehead. Long jet-black hair hung loose from the cap and flowed over the collar of her blue down parka. I'd never seen a girl quite like her before.

"Are you ready for Mount Everest, Mr. Bud?" she said to Bud, smiling. "Or would you prefer to sleep all day?"

"I'm sick," replied Bud.

"Oh no!" exclaimed Pasang, looking disappointed as I described the symptoms.

"Tom's anxious to get A.N.G. up on the glacier," said Bud. He looked over at me. "Do it, man. I'll be okay here." He gave Pasang a sly look. "I can practice cheating at cards."

She grinned. "I'll have my cousin Nawang check on you and make sure you're not crazy." She wiggled her finger in a circle around her ear. "Sometimes people come up here and do odd things."

"Like what?" I asked.

"You don't want to know," she said.

"Oh yes we do," said Bud.

"All right," said Pasang. "Well, if you manage to survive, I'll tell you some high-altitude insanity stories."

"Deal!" yelled Bud.

Then Pasang invited me again to the ceremony up at the Sherpa campsite. "Puja starts in ten minutes," she said with a grin. "Don't be shocked if you see grown men smearing cooked rice on their faces."

"Awesome!" I said, scrambling out of my bag. "I'll be right there."

Thirty minutes later I was chewing on a granola bar and watching Sherpas jump kick A.N.G. across the rocky slope below our campsite.

No, they weren't angry at my Sherpbot anymore (although a few of the attacks were particularly *spirited*). This was a planned test of the robot's innards. When pushed, A.N.G.'s internal gyroscope and laser scanner were programmed to trigger an instant compensating response from its legs in order to maintain balance and footing on uneven terrain.

I'm happy to say my boy passed with flying colors.

"Impressive," said Q.U.I.P. from my watch. "Not bad for a brainless mechanoid."

"A.N.G's not brainless," I said.

"Really?"

"Yes, really," I said.

"When I scan the beast, no intelligence is evident," said Q.U.I.P. somewhat haughtily. *"None whatsoever."*

"If Yo heard you say that, she'd blow a gasket," I said. "Then she'd reprogram you into a toaster oven."

I heard my name called and turned to look up the rocky slope. Pasang and Gombu waved down at me.

"We're ready!" called Pasang.

I waved at her and pulled out a remote control for A.N.G. The sherpbot responded to voice commands, but for tricky micromaneuvers over dangerous terrain, the remote provided a much finer control of his movements.

Looking upslope at the jagged insanity of the icefall above us, I could see that I'd need all the control I could get.

The Khumbu Icefall looks like a flood raging down a steep canyon but frozen in midsurge. As the great mass of the Khumbu Glacier slides down into the valley below, it drops two thousand feet in less than a mile, breaking into a jumbled maze of gaping chasms and unstable ice towers called seracs. As you can imagine, transit is very, very treacherous. In fact more climbers have died in the Khumbu ice than on any other part of Everest.

Gombu and Pasang were skilled guides; indeed Gombu had led more than three hundred trips across the area. But the icefall is a flow that changes daily. Veteran mountaineers always navigate the shifting, chaotic icescape slowly and with extreme caution. One Everest guide I read called it "a two-thousand-vertical-foot jungle gym on steroids."

Amazingly Gombu climbed with a standard aluminum extension ladder strapped across his back.

"Please stay behind me," he said politely. "Try to step only where I step."

"Roger that," I said.

He didn't have to tell me twice. I knew his ladder was for crossing the deep fissures where the icefall was tearing itself apart. Some of these crevasses can drop as far as a hundred feet. Ouch!

A.N.G. plodded along gamely behind us. So far, so good.

Soon we reached a jagged, thirty-feet-high shelf of ice. Wide troughs of bright snow curved around either side of this serac. But Gombu stopped and surveyed the area for several minutes.

"We must climb here," he finally said.

"We can't just walk around it?" I asked.

"No," said Gombu. He pointed at the snow in the troughs. "See how white?"

"Yes," I said. "Is that bad?"

Gombu said, "Good chance to fall through."

Pasang began to uncoil some climbing rope. "Always beware the whiter streaks on a glacier," she added. "Could be an unstable snow bridge over a crevasse."

As Gombu felt around for handholds on the ice wall, Pasang clipped the uncoiled rope to his belt. Then up he went. For an older guy Gombu was unbelievably strong and nimble. He reached the top, about thirty feet up, in just seconds.

Pasang went next, using the rope her father had just anchored at the top. When she dropped the line back down, I clipped it on the ladder and up it went. We repeated the process with A.N.G., and the two Sherpas hauled him up, too.

"Very light!" called Gombu.

It sounded like praise, so I said, "Thanks!"

"Is it an aluminum alloy?" called down Pasang. "Or did you go lighter—magnesium zirconium maybe?"

I was stunned. "How do you know about magnesium alloys?"

Pasang looked down at me from atop the ice shelf. "Well, I go to school," she said dryly.

"What kind of school teaches you about magnesium alloys?" I asked.

"High school," she said.

I laughed. "Wow," I said, shaking my head.

"So it surprises you that Sherpas in Nepal actually take chemistry?" she said.

Uh-oh. "No, no," I said. "No, I just . . . I, uh, I'm . . . I'm . . ." I raised my shoulders and dropped them in defeat. "I'm an idiot, is what I am."

"Well, mister idiot, here's some rope for you," called Pasang. "Don't hang yourself with it." I could hear Gombu chuckling somewhere behind her.

When the line dropped again, I used it to haul myself up the ice face. Even with the rope, the ascent wasn't easy. My awe at Gombu's strength and agility was growing by the minute.

At the top I gave Pasang a wry look. "Sorry," I said.

"That's okay," she said. "I find that I enjoy giving you a hard time."

"She's very smart!" said Gombu with obvious pride.

"I can see that," I said.

"Pasang wants to build spaceships!" he said, glancing up at the sky.

I looked at her. "Really?" I said.

"I'm looking at colleges in the United States with strong aerospace engineering programs," she said.

"Colleges?" I said. "How old are you?"

"Seventeen years," interjected Gombu. "Very smart—*too* smart." He grinned and leaned toward me, lowering his voice. "She gets it from her mother."

Pasang laughed and threw her arm around her father's neck.

I said, "My dad's company does aerospace projects, and we work with university researchers all the time. I'll ask him if he has any advice for you on schools."

Pasang's eyes widened. "That would be wonderful!" she said.

Suddenly a brisk, frigid breeze kicked up a dusting

of snow that swirled around us. The wind's bite instantly made it feel twenty degrees colder. Fortunately I was geared up well for this trek. My insulated, waterproof snowsuit was made of breathable Swift-Tex fabric. My polar gloves were superwarm too, plus they had a little modification that I'd designed with help from the guys in the Swift Enterprises materials lab: conductive silver alloy fingertips. These let me operate A.N.G.'s remote control device without having to remove gloves in the brutal Himalayan cold.

Despite the extreme conditions and difficult trail, A.N.G. performed quite well—at first, anyway.

The Sherpbot trotted nimbly through the jutting, uneven ice and snow, all while carrying over a hundred pounds of gear, including my snowboard and Swift-Foil kite. My goal was to get above the Khumbu Icefall and then climb another thousand feet up the flat, powder-filled basin of the Western Cwm. There I could snow-kite around for a while, then kite back down to the upper icefall. We'd descend to Base Camp for another night of acclimation.

As we reached the upper icefall—the jumbled area

known to climbers as the Popcorn—the terrain got steeper and more twisted. Suddenly, for no apparent reason, A.N.G. lost its balance as it slalomed through a jumble of ice blocks. The Sherpbot landed on its side, slid down a smooth slab of ice, and slammed into the base of a white, twisted serac that looked like a tortured gargoyle.

The impact set the big tower wobbling.

"Oh crud," I said, frozen by indecision. I wanted badly to leap down the slab to retrieve A.N.G. But the ice tower suddenly gave out a strange groan.

"Watch out!" warned Pasang.

In a split second the tower collapsed. At first it dropped straight down, collapsing upon itself, but then its top half teetered toward us.

"Move!" shouted Gombu.

"Here!" cried Pasang at the same time.

Both moved so fast that they looked like jungle cats springing at prey. Dropping his ladder, Gombu seized my arm and pulled me off the ice block where we stood. I found myself falling right into a snow drift, crunching through its surface crust, then sinking nearly knee deep into the powder underneath. Pasang landed softly next to me . . . and

I heard the chilling, explosive *crack* of ice shattering above us.

"Duck!" she screamed.

And then I was hammered by what felt like a million ice cubes.

6

Call of the Wild

The boom and clatter of an ice collapse is something I never want to hear again. But the dead silence afterward . . . now *that* was scary.

Why? Because I wasn't sure I was alive.

For several seconds I lay curled in a ball, seeing nothing but gray light and feeling a heavy weight on my back. Then with a rush of raw energy and fear, I pushed upward with my hands.

Whew! I burst up through a few inches of ice and snow layered atop me.

Next to me, Pasang and Gombu popped up too.

"You okay?" I asked.

As Pasang nodded, Gombu was already moving his hands over the sheer cliff face. We were at the bottom of a small crevasse, maybe fifteen feet deep on the near side where the ice tower collapsed but much higher on the opposite side.

"Can we get out?" I asked.

Neither of them answered.

Pasang's eyes were dark with concern as she brushed snow and ice debris off her parka. Then her eyes lit up; she pointed at the ground nearby and said something sharply in her native language. Gombu spun around.

I looked down too.

"The ladder!" I said.

The tip of Gombu's aluminum ladder jutted through the snow. The serac collapse had washed it over the ledge. Good thing it hadn't landed on one of us. We immediately began scraping and digging away the debris, then yanked the ladder free.

After that it was a simple matter to climb out of the chasm.

As we scrambled over the broken chunks of ice, I was stunned to find A.N.G. standing atop the ice rubble down near the base of where the fallen serac had once stood. My Sherpbot had somehow emerged from the collapse undamaged—or so I thought at first.

"A.N.G., heel!" I called down.

A.N.G. started bouncing in circles.

We stared at it for a second. Then Gombu started to laugh.

"Your Sherpa is dancing!" he cried.

Maybe it was the exhilaration of just being alive, but I found myself laughing too. I looked over at Pasang, and we laughed hard. When I finally caught my breath, I heaved a big sigh of relief.

"Wow," I said.

"Yes, wow," agreed Pasang.

"Wow squared," said Q.U.I.P. on my wrist.

"It appears our robot has lost its mind," I said.

"Trust me," said Q.U.I.P. "It had no mind to lose in the first place."

As Pasang scooted carefully down the ice slab toward A.N.G., she asked, "Why did it fall?"

"I don't know," I said, puzzled. "This ice field is no trickier than most of the others we crossed where he did just fine." I slid slowly down behind Pasang until we both stood next to the hopping, circling Sherpbot. Then I called out, "A.N.G., halt!"

A.N.G. just kept dancing.

I tried the remote control. No luck. The control

program had crashed and was caught in a repeating loop.

"Grab his legs," I said to Pasang.

"What?"

"His legs," I said. "Grab them. Then we'll flip him on his back so I can do a manual shutdown."

I dove down and tackled A.N.G.'s back legs. Pasang, following my lead, tried to wrap up his front legs. A.N.G. is pretty strong, of course, so the struggle to wrap up dancing hydraulic legs was pretty desperate for a few seconds.

Above us on the slab, Gombu laughed in delight.

"Is this the mountain rodeo?" he called.

We finally flipped A.N.G., and, avoiding his thrashing legs, I slid open a small hatch and punched a manual override button. A.N.G. froze in place.

"Now what?" asked Pasang.

"I was afraid you'd ask that," I replied.

Obviously A.N.G. still had some bugs that needed fixing. For this testing phase Yo had insisted on installing a high-capacity data drive in A.N.G.'s head module. She'd wanted the robot to log everything it processed during its prototype stages so she could review the code and make adjustments if necessary.

All I had to do was upload the last three hours of debug data to Yo back in New York. Maybe she could figure out what went wrong in the navigational programming. But to do this, we'd have to get A.N.G. back down to Base Camp and plug into my campsite's communications dome.

"How close is the top of the icefall?" I asked.

"Very close," said Gombu.

"Twenty, thirty minutes maybe," added Pasang, "if the ice is stable."

The wind had stopped, and now the late morning sun was starting to warm up the glacier. I could hear groans and cracks all around. I looked down at ANG.

"If we can get this guy up to Camp I, I could probably get my hovercraft in there for a pickup," I said.

"No problem," said Gombu.

I stared at him. "No problem?" I repeated.

"Rope," he said to Pasang.

She immediately uncoiled more climbing rope. Soon, to my amazement, we had A.N.G. strapped onto Gombu's back. I loaded some of the gear A.N.G. had been carrying, including the folded foil-kite, into my backpack; Pasang stashed the rest in hers.

"You look like a monster from outer space," said Pasang with a laugh as her father led us over the last few ice boulders at the top of the icefall. With A.N.G.'s four legs sticking out from his back, he did resemble some sort of weird extraterrestrial creature.

"I'm very happy," replied Gombu. He stopped and looked around at me. "Because your monster is very light."

"Hey, he's not *that* light," I said in admiration. "You're amazing, sirdar."

I addressed him by his leadership title. This seemed to please him. He bowed and continued upward.

Soon we emerged from the falling ice mass into the large snowy valley known as the Western Cwm. I was happy to leave the Khumbu Icefall behind for now. I knew we'd be back through tomorrow, but I was ready for some of the highest snow-kiting ever.

"Cwm" is a Welsh word for a cirque, which is a bowl-shaped glacial valley enclosed by high mountain walls. After the tense, cramped insanity of the icefall, the white expanse of the Western Cwm opened up above us like a vision of paradise. Half a mile wide, it extends almost two miles up the valley beneath the southwest face of Everest.

"The Valley of Silence," murmured Gombu reverently.

"It's beautiful!" I cried out.

"Yes, but don't be lulled into careless climbing," warned Pasang. "Still plenty of crevasses everywhere."

"First camp just ahead," said Gombu.

Sure enough, a small encampment of tents and storage shelters lay scattered across the snow not far above where the icefall began its drop. This was Camp I, which sits at 19,500 feet above sea level.

"Do you feel good?" Gombu asked me as we approached.

"I do," I said. "I feel *great*."

I play sports year-round at school, so I'm in good shape. But even top athletes can suffer from mountain sickness; reactions to altitude can vary wildly from person to person. Fortunately my body seemed to be adapting quite well.

"So, you think you can make it to second camp?" asked Pasang.

"Absolutely," I said.

"Then we take a short rest here," said Gombu.

We ate a light lunch, drank a lot of fluids, and relaxed for about forty-five minutes. Then we prepared to set off again, leaving A.N.G. behind. Some of the Sherpa porters who were stocking Camp I for the summit climbing teams got a kick out of seeing the odd robot.

"Do we guard it?" called one young porter. "Or does it guard us?"

Another one said, "Don't worry, we'll keep it fed."

I grinned and bowed. "Thanks," I said.

Our next destination was Camp II at 21,000 feet—a relatively easy, if slow and uneventful, hike up the snowy valley. This camp is pitched near the imposing Lhotse Face, a wall of glacial blue ice rising sharply 3,700 feet. Sometimes called Advanced Base Camp, Camp II is big and usually well stocked with supplies, since it is the final launch point for all summit attempts.

We reached Camp II in just under three hours. As I unloaded my gear, I glanced up at a spectacular view of snow plumes blowing off the Everest summit eight thousand feet above us. It seemed so close, yet so far.

Pasang noticed my gaze. "Shall we go for the top?" she said, grinning.

"Maybe some day," I said.

"It's a very difficult climb," she said. "But not impossible."

"Have you been up there?" I said, nodding at the summit.

"Once," she said.

"What was it like?"

She paused, and then said, "Like nothing else."

"I'll bet."

This stop at Camp II was definitely as far as I planned to go. I knew that a Mount Everest summit attempt required weeks of heavy-duty preparation and training. Summiteers must spend many days acclimating on the mountain itself, going up and down repeatedly to get the body used to the altitude. My trip goal was to test A.N.G. on the highest mountain in the world, not to test myself. I wasn't even remotely ready for the summit of Everest; I knew that.

But I *did* want to get in some primo snow-kiting.

The weather was considerably warmer on the open, sun-drenched Western Cym than elsewhere on the mountain, and I noticed Pasang peeling off her blue parka. Then I got a wild idea.

As she kneeled over her pack to stuff in the coat, I scooped up a big, mushy snowball. Hey, I owed her one, right? After a big-league windup, I fired a fastball right at her backside.

"Ow!" she screamed. "Hey!"

Spinning to glare at me, she bared her teeth.

I shrugged. "Ooops!" I said.

And then it was war: a full-scale snowball battle at 21,000 feet. I tagged her good a couple of times, and vice versa. Maybe the lack of oxygen had something to do with it, but we were shrieking and laughing like hyenas. We chased each other upslope another five hundred feet to the base of the steep, blue Lhotse Face.

And then it happened.

As I ducked an attack by diving behind a mound of rock, I caught sight of what looked like a row of sinkholes in the nearby snow. The spacing looked too regular to be random, so I concluded it must be a line of footprints.

When I crawled over, keeping low to avoid getting tagged by snowballs, I discovered I was right: They *were* footprints.

"Pasang!" I shouted. "Get over here! *Now!*"

My nemesis had her arm cocked, ready to zing another missile. But when she heard my voice, she dropped it and sprinted over.

We looked down at the set of tracks. They were huge—at least twice the size of my own size-ten boot tracks.

And . . . they appeared to be a barefoot human.

"Five toes," I said, pointing. "Long, flat heel."

Pasang gave me a frightened look. *"Dzu-teh,"* she said.

"What?" I said.

"Dzu-teh," she repeated. "Giant." She looked down at the prints again. "Yeti."

Off in the distance, coming from up high on the Lhotse Face, we heard a high-pitched chirp or whistle. It warbled slightly and then deepened. It ended in a bone-chilling howl.

Yeti Tales

Suddenly my little expedition to Mount Everest had a whole new agenda.

Two hours later, after our return trip down the glacier to Camp I, I sat with Gombu and Pasang in front of our newly pitched tents just above the icefall. I was talking to Bud via my F14 portable radio.

Bud's voice crackled over the transceiver: "Let me confirm this item list. Over."

I adjusted the clip-on microphone on my collar and replied, "Shoot it at me, bro. Over."

We'd descended the Western Cwm quickly after making our discovery. The sun was sinking behind the towering peaks to the west and a deeper chill had settled across the glacial valley. Our plans were to spend the night at Camp I, then descend the icefall to Base Camp in the morning.

"So you want five sets of night-vision goggles," said Bud.

"Check," I said.

"One DNA sample collection kit," he said.

"Check."

"Two dozen remote, wireless, infrared motion detectors, plus network control pod," said Bud.

"Correct."

"Ten sixteen-megapixel digital cameras with remote control and additional data sticks for picture storage," he said.

"Yes," I confirmed.

"And a partridge in a pear tree."

I grinned. "That's the key component," I said.

"Yes, it really links the whole system together," said Bud. With a hint of skepticism, he added, "Now, Tom, you're sure Swift Enterprises will just round up all this advanced gear and ship it right to the Base Camp of Mount Everest?"

"As long as your request goes directly to Dr. Rashid," I said. "Just be sure to key in the order code I gave you. Then he'll know it's from me."

Dr. Victor Rashid was the lab director and head scientist at my dad's company. He's one of the smartest guys I know, and he usually comes through for me, even when my equipment requests are a little, shall we say, extravagant. He trusts me.

"Okay, well, I've got your PDA fired up," replied Bud. "I'll send off this request immediately."

"Thanks, dude," I said. "See you in the morning. How are you feeling, by the way?"

"Much better, thanks," he said. "I've had trekkers and guides checking in on me, bringing me really strange food." He paused. "I've been hiding food all day so I don't hurt anybody's feelings."

This brought a thin smile to Pasang's face . . . finally. She'd been mostly silent since we found the footprints, and I could tell she was troubled. Gombu was all business too. I caught him looking over at his daughter several times, keeping an eye on her.

"Okay, good buddy," I said into the microphone. "Over and out."

"Roger, out," replied Bud.

I unzipped my tent and invited my companions inside for tea. They graciously accepted, so I scooped some snow into my ultralight anodized kettle and popped it on my propane camp stove. In just minutes we were sipping aromatic Nepalese tea.

Darkness was rapidly gathering now, so I fired up a small krypton lantern.

"Pasang," I said. "Are you okay?"

"Yes," she said, looking into her teacup.

Gombu's dark eyes glittered in the lamplight. "My daughter is smart, but she believes in the old tales," he said. "The *dzu-teh* has been seen many times in the high passes."

"I know," I said. "I've read some of the stories."

"Sherpas have stories," said Gombu. "But not only Sherpas, you know."

"Climbers have reported yeti sightings," said Pasang quietly, shrugging. "Everybody knows that." She looked at me. "Those you've read, I'm sure. But lately the guides have seen more signs."

"What kind of signs?" I asked. I was starting to feel a little spooked. "Footprints?"

Pasang nodded. "And disturbances," she said.

"Disturbances?"

"Yes," she said. "Movements."

Suddenly, outside, I heard a rumble far up the valley. It was an avalanche; I could hear the tumbling rock and the weird hissing flow of the snow surge. We were right in the valley's center, almost a quarter mile from either ridge, so only a catastrophic break in the mountain's face could reach us. But it was a distant reminder of Everest's ever-lurking danger.

I felt pretty tired all of a sudden. The trip up the glacier and back had taken more out of me than I thought. I looked down at my own teacup. It felt heavy.

"Sleep well," said Gombu, seeing my exhaustion.

He motioned to his daughter and they left for their tents. As they pushed open the flap, I saw A.N.G. just outside. Even though my robot was little more than a glorified statue at this point, it felt oddly comforting to have him "standing guard" just outside.

Gombu turned and looked at me through the flap.

"There is an old Sherpa saying," he said. "You might wish to remember it."

I nodded. "What is it, Gombu?"

"The old Sherpa lama once said this," he said. "'There is a yeti in the back of everyone's mind; only the blessed are not haunted by it.'" He smiled at me. "You know what the yeti is, don't you?"

"No," I said. "What is it?"

Gombu gave me a look. "Fear," he said.

And off he went. I pushed into my sleeping bag. Then I slept like a rock for almost twelve hours.

The return trip down the Khumbu Icefall was uneventful.

I'd warned Bud to stay mum about the mystery footprints, but other Sherpa guides had spotted them too, and news had already spread through the Base Camp by the time we arrived. Sherpas were less outgoing; some even seemed grim. Mountaineers peppered me with questions. I tried to downplay the discovery, but the buzz continued throughout the day.

I felt less fatigued, and Bud was looking much better too. But we decided to follow the usual acclimation method and stay at Base Camp for at least one more full night. The gear I'd requested wouldn't arrive until the next day anyway, so I fired up the Sub-Orbiter for a quick trip to retrieve A.N.G. from Camp I, then came back to Base Camp.

Sometime in the early afternoon, my PDA beeped with an incoming call. It was Yo.

"Hey, dude," I said. "How's the family?"

"Big," she said.

"Having fun?" I asked.

"It's a party," she replied. "How about you?"

"Things are . . . very interesting here," I said.

"So I've heard," she said. "I've got a bug fix for you."

"For A.N.G.?"

"Yep," she said. "I'm uploading a patch right now."

"Sweet!" I exclaimed. "What was the problem?"

"I found an infinite loop in the source code," she said. "That 'circle dance' A.N.G. did is an escape maneuver for certain situations—in particular, when he loses all traction, which I'm guessing is what happened."

"Good guess," I said. "He was crossing a very slick ice slab."

"Anyway, A.N.G. got stuck in the loop because my lame code didn't give him a way out." She paused. "Aren't you going to mock me, Swift?"

"Maybe later," I said with a grin.

"Well, let me know how it works," she said. "For now a simple reboot should get him moving again."

I slapped my forehead. "Of course!" I said. "I should have tried rebooting instead of making Gombu carry a seventy-five pound robot on his back up a flipping glacier."

"No, actually, you were right," said Yo. "The way he's programmed now, A.N.G. probably would have just gotten caught in a loop again. But this patch should fix it for you."

"Thanks, man," I said.

"Good luck," she said. "Hey, I hear you made friends with a hot Sherpa girl."

"What?" I almost yelled.

Yo chuckled. "Yeah, Bud says she's smart and cute and he can tell she likes you."

"She's not that cute," I lied.

"Right."

"Hey, Pasang is my *guide*," I said.

"I'll bet she is," said Yo.

"Leave me alone," I said, turning red I'm sure. Yo liked to give me a hard time about all kinds of things, especially other girls.

"Okay, okay," laughed Yo. "By the way, my computer now says the patch is fully uploaded. Go for it, dog."

"Okay," I said.

"Adios."

"Yeah, adios."

Sure enough, my PDA gave its "e-mail received"

chime, and I found a rather large bug patch attached. Yo had also attached a text file with instructions. It looked like the fix would take a few hours because of built-in diagnostic routines that would run, so I wouldn't have time to physically test A.N.G. up on the glacier or anywhere else that day.

So Bud and I broke out the cards again.

The Australian climbing team—the one Gombu was head guide for—wasn't going to the summit for a few more days because of a late shipment of oxygen canisters. So we convinced a few of that team's younger Sherpas to join us for some Slapjack. I couldn't find Pasang, though.

After hours of loud, spirited play by lamplight, plus tales of yeti sightings and other local folklore, we called it a night.

"Some of those yeti stories are pretty horrifying," said Bud as he zipped up his sleeping bag. "Dudes nine feet tall leaving half-eaten yaks behind . . ." He shivered. "No wonder yaks are so hostile around here."

"Yaks aren't hostile," I said, trying not to laugh.

"They look hostile," said Bud sleepily.

"I'll grant you that," I said, smiling. "But don't you

find it interesting that at a lot of the stories were about yetis *helping* people."

It was true.

As I lay in the tent listening to Bud snore, I heard the thrumming of a helicopter again, like I'd heard the first night at Base Camp. As before, it was whisper quiet, as helicopters go. But then a breeze kicked up, and the sound faded behind the wind's moan.

I crawled to the front flap, opened it, and peeked out into the night. Nothing.

I don't remember falling asleep, but I remember the nightmare from which I jolted awake in a sweat. In the dream I was on a creamy white sand beach. It was hot. I started to walk out into the blue green surf.

Suddenly huge tentacles burst from the sand.

Everybody on the beach was yelling, *"The kraken! The kraken!"*

8

The Blue Wasp

The next morning, Base Camp was bigger. And my jet-black Swift Sub-Orbiter had a cobalt blue companion.

When Bud and I opened our tent flap, we looked out on a new cluster of tents: eight blue alpine shelters, all pitched in the night, apparently. Farther down the slope, near the Sub-Orbiter, sat the blue helicopter we'd seen back at Lukla airfield.

"The yak hunters!" exclaimed Bud.

I whipped out my Konica eight-by-twenty-four mini binoculars and surveyed their village.

"Check out that gear," I said.

All kinds of gleaming high-tech equipment lay spread out on a canvas tarp by the tents. Two men in bush hats were checking and sorting the stuff. In general, it looked like communication and detection gear—everything from portable radios and high-power Maglite LED flashlights to laser rangefinders and something that looked like a small, silver radar dish.

Arrayed near one of the tents was a row of three high-power sniper rifles, each with a telescopic sight attached to a long barrel. I handed the mini binoculars to Bud.

"Who *are* these guys?" I asked.

"They've got some serious cash financing, whoever they are," said Bud, focusing on the gear.

"The rifles alone are probably ten thousand dollars apiece," I said.

"That's nuts," said Bud.

"Somehow, I don't think they're yak hunters, dude," I said. "You don't have to shoot a yak from eleven hundred meters with a scope. Those weapons are for more *elusive* game."

Bud gave me a wide-eyed look. "Yeti hunters?"

"That would be my guess," I said.

"Wait a minute," said Bud. "Aren't yeti—*if* they exist—some early form of hominid, maybe even related to humans?"

"That's the theory," I said.

"So, then shooting one would be sort of like . . . murder," he said.

"Especially if some of the Sherpa stories are true," I agreed.

Blinking in the sunlight, we stepped out of our tent's vestibule. Bud shook his head at the sight of the blue helicopter down the hill.

"It *does* look like a wasp," he said.

Then I noticed a tall fierce-looking man in a blue bush hat—the same man I'd seen sitting in the helicopter at Lukla. He was walking up the hill toward the new tent village pitched just a hundred feet or so from us. But then he spotted us standing there . . . and abruptly veered toward us.

"Uh-oh," said Bud.

"What's wrong?" I asked.

"He's coming!"

"So?"

Bud rubbed his hands together nervously. "Maybe we're in trouble?"

I squinted at him. "Why?"

"Uh, because . . . because we're kids, and he's not?"

This made me laugh. I was laughing when the man walked up and nodded at me.

"Having fun?" he asked. His voice was a deep bass rumble, and there was a slight hint of mockery in it.

"Yes sir, I am, actually," I said.

"Good," he said. "You're Tom Swift," he added—a statement, not a query, almost as if he was bestowing my name upon me.

He extended his large hand and I shook it; his grip was quite powerful.

"Who are you?" blurted Bud.

When nervous, Bud is a blurter. Normally he's a very respectful kid. But when he's anxious, he tends to blurt what's on his mind. The man considered Bud briefly, then quickly dismissed him. He turned his dark gaze to me again.

"My name is Jackson Mallory," he said. He paused as if waiting for a reaction.

"Hello," I said.

"Yes," said Mallory. "Can we talk?"

"Sure," I said. "What about?" I was pretty sure I knew the topic.

"Your discovery at the Lhotse Face," he said.

I nodded. Bud brought out our two folding camp chairs and set them up, then said, "I have to talk to Gombu about something. I'll catch you later."

"See you, dude," I said.

Bud bowed briefly to Mallory, then headed uphill to the expedition tents. As he left, the man and I both sat in the camp chairs.

"There's really not much to tell you, Mr. Mallory," I said. "We found some footprints—humanlike, but huge." I shrugged. "That's about it."

Mallory nodded slowly. "Did you document these tracks?" he asked.

"They weren't *tracks*," I said. "They were footprints."

Mallory narrowed his dark eyes. "Did you document them?" he asked again, his voice lower.

"You mean, like, take photos?" I asked. "No."

"Did you measure them?"

"No."

"Scan them?"

"No."

"Take samples?"

I shook my head. "I didn't have a collection kit with me," I said. "I didn't have anything like that. I mean, I wasn't out there *hunting for yeti*."

I delivered this last sentence a bit harshly. I didn't mean to, but it just sort of slipped out that way. Mallory gave me a long hard look. Then he leaned back in his chair and gazed around Base Camp. Again he seemed like a man comfortable with making people wait while he formulated deep, important thoughts.

Finally he nodded down the hill. "That's the famous Swift sub-orbital craft," he said.

"Yes," I said.

"Where's your pilot?" he asked, trying to sound casual.

"I'm the pilot," I said.

"You?" Mallory gave a deep little chuckle.

I didn't respond. The guy was starting to get on my nerves.

Mallory stood up. He looked down at me in a way that seemed to emphasize his great size. He said, "Mr. Swift, I can see you're no fool."

"Hey, thanks," I said. I stood up too. I didn't like the way he was hovering over me . . . like a condor examining a carcass.

"I've been hunting big game since I was your age, maybe even younger," he said. He got a wistful look in his eye and glanced up at Everest looming above us. "I've tracked and bagged some of the rarest, most beautiful creatures known to man."

"You *bagged* them?" I repeated.

"Yes," he said. "And now I've been hired to investigate reports of the rarest creature of them all. It seems you've found evidence that perhaps this creature not only exists, but may be roaming just up there, just above us"—he pointed toward the Lhotse Face—"even now, even as we speak."

"I don't think you were hired to *investigate* this thing, Mr. Mallory," I said. "You were hired to *bag* it."

Mallory smiled just enough that I could see the pointy tips of his two canine teeth.

"My employer wants a yeti sample," he said, "dead or alive."

I just stood there with my arms folded across my chest.

"So, my question to you, Mr. Swift, is this," he said. "Do you plan to . . . *investigate* your finding further?"

"Yes I do," I said.

"And I suspect you'll bring in some of the resources available to you from Swift Enterprises?" he said. "Your father's laboratories?"

"Maybe," I said.

Mallory smiled again. "I don't suppose you'd consider working together with me on this," he said.

He gestured toward his camp down the slope. "Our combined assets would be formidable."

I answered without hesitation.

"Not a chance," I said.

Mallory's eyes grew icy cold. It was a scary transformation, I must say.

"Very well," he said.

And then without a handshake, a look, or another word, the big man turned and walked away.

Thirty minutes later, Bud tapped excitedly on the keyboard of my PDA.

"Dude, *he's* the Blue Wasp!" said Bud as he read something onscreen. "The tool named his helicopter after himself."

"You're kidding," I said.

"No," said Bud. "Listen. This article says, 'Jackson Mallory uses the latest technology to track and tag his prey. This much is certain: When the Blue Wasp is on the hunt, there is no escaping his sting.'" Bud gave me a sour look. "Boy, as a journalist, I find that last sentence an embarrassment to the craft."

I grinned. "The Blue Wasp, eh?"

"Pretty pompous, if you ask me," said Bud.

"I'd wager good money that Mallory came up with the name himself," I said.

Bud laughed. "I wouldn't take that bet."

Dad always says you should know your competitor better than you know yourself. So Bud and I did a little Internet research on Jackson Mallory. It confirmed what he'd told me: He was a world-famous big-game hunter.

But our research also revealed something Mallory *hadn't* told me: His primary employer over the years had been none other than Foger Utility Group. That's right, FUG, the number-one rival of my dad's company. For many years, FUG has been trying to steal Swift secrets, sabotage Swift products, and damage the Swift reputation.

"FUG," I said, shaking my head. "That probably explains why he knows about Swift Enterprises and my so-called resources. Ah, speaking of which . . ."

Outside the tent I could hear the loud rotor thump and whine of a helicopter. Bud and I hurried outside to see a red Bell 407 dropping into the valley.

"That's our bird," I said, excited.

Yes, thanks to the resources of Swift Enterprises, the yeti-tracking equipment I'd ordered had arrived within twenty-four hours. As Bud and I hiked down the slope to the landing site, I saw Pasang coming downhill to join us. Bud and I both high-fived her. Soon the three of us were unloading the Bell's cargo delivery and transferring it directly into the Sub-Orbiter's hold.

Next Bud and I broke down our tent and communications dome and loaded all that gear into the Sub-Orbiter too. Meanwhile Pasang fetched Gombu and they loaded their tent and stuff too. Finally we all hopped aboard and made the short flight over the icefall and up the glacier to Camp II at the upper end of the Western Cwm—near the spot we'd discovered the odd footprints.

As I pulled my snowboard and folded foil-kite out of the cargo compartment, Gombu noted them and said, "I was with a team on north-side climb in 2001. We were up on the face, and we look up, see a young French man on that." He pointed at my board.

"On a *snowboard*?" said Bud.

"Coming down," said Gombu. He shot his hand out and made a whooshing sound.

"You're kidding, right?" I said.

"No," said Pasang, hefting a pack of camp supplies

93

from the hold. "This man, he was only twenty-three. He rode his board from the summit down the North Col corridor, seventeen thousand feet, all the way to Base Camp."

"That's seriously *sick!*" exclaimed Bud. "Wow!"

"First-ever snowboard descent, top to bottom," said Pasang.

I got excited. "So it's actually possible to board down Everest? All the way?"

Pasang gave me a look. "Oh yes, it's possible," she said.

"I'd love to give that a shot," I said.

Pasang nodded. "Of course, the same Frenchman tried again the very next year. He called his friends from the summit, then rode down the Hornbein Couloir on the north face." She slung her pack to the ground. "They never found him."

I nodded. "Okay," I said. "Maybe not."

After we finished pitching our tents and setting up the Geo-Dome at the new altitude, Bud felt a twinge of headache—it *was* 3,500 feet higher than Base Camp, after all. So we made him rest and drink tea with Gombu while Pasang, and I spent a couple of hours setting up the motion detectors and remote-control cameras around the camp, all the way up to the base of the Lhotse Face where we'd spotted the footprints.

If the yeti came back, I wanted good pictures of the fellow.

Several times as we moved along the ice wall of the Lhotse Face, we caught sight of the Blue Wasp hovering high above us.

Later, sitting in the tent to eat the meal we'd cooked outside, our talk turned to avalanches. The steep Lhotse Face nearby usually sends down several deadly slides a year.

"Most people think climbers die on Everest by falling off the mountain," said Pasang. "The true fact is that the number-one cause of fatalities on this mountain is avalanche."

Outside, we heard the now familiar thrum of Mallory's helicopter.

"I'm sure the Blue Wasp is keeping a close eye on our operation," said Bud with a sly grin.

"Yeah, he hovered over us half the afternoon," I said darkly. "No doubt scanning the southwest face with infrared detectors, looking for thermal images of the yeti."

"Why doesn't he just land that thing and trek like a man?" said Bud.

Pasang gave him a solid knuckle whap on the arm.

"Ow!" said Bud. "Sorry."

I grinned. "Pasang could probably carry you down this mountain on her back," I said.

She shook her head. "No," she said. "Actually I'd leave him to rot."

Bud dug into his pocket.

"Cards, anyone?" he said.

"I would like to learn these cards," said Gombu. "It seems everyone enjoys them. Or am I too old?"

I laughed. "No, sirdar," I said. "I play cards with my father all the time."

"Excellent!" said Gombu, raising his eyebrows. "Then teach me!"

Every few rounds of Hearts, we would hear the Blue Wasp make another pass over the faces of Everest and Lhotse. As darkness fell and the temperature dropped, I fired up my catalytic heater. We talked and laughed and laid down cards by the orange lantern light.

When it finally came time to say good night, Bud

conked out almost immediately. But I found myself staring up at the tent's dark vented roof, unable to sleep for quite some time.

I listened for the odd warbling call followed by a howl that I'd heard when Pasang and I found the footprints the day before. I listened for crunching snow—the footfall of a nine-feet-tall man-beast, the *dzu-teh*. Did he really exist?

I listened and waited.

But I heard nothing, not even the usual moan of the Everest winds.

9

Big Downhill Ride

Early the next morning, I awoke to the sound of aluminum cooking pots banging together. Bud sat bolt upright at the sound.

"What the hey?" he exclaimed.

"Get up, campers!" cried Pasang just outside our tent.

"What is it?" I called.

"We had a visitor last night," she replied.

Bud and I exchanged a wild look. Then we scrambled into our clothes and out of the tent.

Sure enough, just up the slope a trail of large barefoot prints led right up the steep, snowy grade of the Lhotse Face. These prints looked slightly different from the ones we'd found before: several inches shorter overall, with fatter toe pads and a narrower, more curved heel.

"Could this be a second yeti?" asked Pasang.

"Maybe," I said.

Bud is more skeptical by nature than I am. "Or maybe they're fake," he said. "We know Mallory's team has been lurking around. Maybe they're trying to throw us off the trail or discredit us or something."

"I guess that's always a possibility, knowing what kind of fellow he is," I said.

"But look at this stride," said Pasang. She pointed out the distance between prints once they reached the sharp upward incline of the mountain's face. "It's enormous! No normal human could run uphill with a stride measurement like that."

"Good point," I said. I stepped off almost eight uphill paces between each footprint. "Yes, that's pretty insane." I hopped back down to the bottom of the snow-covered ice wall. "It looks like he got spooked right about here . . . and then really started hauling it uphill."

It was pretty amazing—and a bit scary—to see the evidence of such a huge, powerful creature.

Pasang, Gombu, and I set out to follow the tracks while Bud stayed back at Camp II with some other

Sherpas who'd joined us. Since we weren't yetis, we donned crampons—metal spikes that you attach to your boots—in order to climb the Lhotse Face. You literally kick the spikes through the surface snow into the hard blue ice beneath on every step you take. It's a slow and grueling process, but it's better than slipping a thousand feet or more down the steep ice wall.

Gombu, of course, took the lead, fixing the ropes on a route running next to the yeti prints. We pulled and kicked our way up behind him, digging in our crampons. After maybe two hours of this I started to feel a great heaviness.

I turned back to look at Pasang.

"I can't make it," I said.

She stepped closer and pushed my climbing goggles up onto my forehead. Then she looked into my eyes. "Tell me about the properties of magnesium alloy."

I was confused. I squinted at her. "What?"

"Explain how you patched your robot," she said.

I just looked at her. I couldn't think. Suddenly I was overwhelmed by a funny feeling: *I just don't care.* I kneeled down.

Pasang nodded at me and called ahead to her father. They had a quick exchange in their native language. Then she looked at me and said, "Camp Three is another hour at least, at the speed we're traveling. We can go back down, but first try this."

Leaning into the almost sixty-degree angle of the ice wall, she slung off her pack and pulled out an oxygen mask and cylinder. She helped me strap it on. Then she turned the flow rate up to 1.5 liters per minute.

I felt an immediate surge of happiness and energy. I took deep, hungry breaths, feeling almost guilty that this air "tasted" so good.

"I can go on," I said.

"Just relax a few minutes," said Pasang. "Give yourself some time."

And then I heard the sound again: the rumbling and the hissing surge.

"Avalanche!" cried Gombu.

With a deafening roar, a massive wall of snow slid down the mountain toward us. We had mere seconds to react, with no escape possible. I knew what to do; my backcountry ski training took over. But in the face of such power, it seemed entirely hopeless.

First I whipped off my pack and flung away my walking poles. Your own gear can be one of the most dangerous projectiles in the fall, plus it can drag you under the flow. Then I crouched low against the slope and turned away from the approaching snow mass. When the front edge hit, it was too powerful—I was swept directly downhill. I began "swimming" on top of the flow, stroking my arms; whenever I started tumbling, I kicked hard toward the surface, keeping my mouth clamped shut.

Fortunately the snow was fairly wet, and thus slower moving. A dry snow avalanche travels up to 120 mph and can hit you with the concussive force of an explosive. But this slide was moving only thirty mph or so—fast enough to keep me spinning, but not fast enough to break my bones on impact. As I rolled and swam, my oxygen cylinder and mask were ripped off.

The fall went on and on, but fortunately the Lhotse Face ice wall was a sheer, clean slide for the snow. My fall line was free of boulders, trees, and other objects that could kill me instantly if I struck them. As the avalanche slowed, I was fit and alert enough to follow the basic survival procedures I'd learned. I quickly pulled my hands and arms over my face to form an air pocket.

Friction makes avalanche snow heat up and thicken as it falls until it's like wet cement. If you're buried more than a couple of feet deep, it's almost impossible to move your limbs. When movement finally stopped, I was buried, but when I tried to thrust my arms upward, the left one moved, showing I wasn't buried too deep.

I quickly assessed my situation and figured out that I'd come to rest on my right side in a curled position. My legs were wedged tight, and my right wrist ached. But with another punch, my left arm burst through the white surface, giving me a glorious glimpse of blue sky.

I was alive *and* sitting shallow! I felt an amazing sense of exhilaration.

I kept working my free arm in a circle, again and again, widening its range of motion by scooping out heavy handfuls of the thick wet snow. Soon I'd dug out my left shoulder and my head, then started working on my sore right arm. It was hard, slow work, but eventually I got it free. After that it took just a few more minutes to extricate my lower body from the snow pile.

I rose shakily and took a quick inventory of my body parts. My right wrist ached, but I could move it. Other than that, nothing felt broken or sprained. Ha! It seemed like a miracle. Nothing else even hurt, other than a few minor bumps and bruises.

I held up my sore wrist and said, "Q.U.I.P.? Hello, Q.U.I.P.? Are you there?"

No response. I pulled up my sleeve and found my minicom watch completely smashed. *Must have slammed into a rock or something,* I thought. No wonder my wrist hurt.

Then I stood up and took my first look at the "run-out zone"—the area where the heaviest debris (in this case, mostly snow) comes to rest. It was a stunning sight. I was standing in the Western Cwm! I looked up; the avalanche track running down the Lhotse Face was at least a fifty yards wide. It had dumped the outflow debris (including me) down into the glacial valley, a thousand feet below.

In fact I now stood less than a quarter mile from Camp II, the place I'd left two hours earlier. What a return trip. I'd come back down in roughly sixty seconds by body-surfing a great white wave.

I was incredibly lucky to be alive. For a second I felt giddy.

But then it hit me. My companions!

"Pasang!" I called. "Gombu!"

I clambered across the deposition pile—the ridge of debris where the piled snow was deepest—looking for signs of them. I knew the first fifteen minutes were critical. After that chances of survival drop quickly for survivors buried in an avalanche. I scrambled over the great mounds of snow, yelling out their names, listening for signs of life.

For an hour, I searched. No luck.

Now fatigue was setting in again, and the sun had dropped behind the mountain. I realized I'd better trek back to Bud at Camp II. If I didn't reach shelter before nightfall, I was dead, cold meat. I could already feel the chill of the gathering darkness seeping into my bones. Time was running short.

Then I saw an arm jutting from the snow. Unmoving.

I dived to the spot and started digging furiously. As I uncovered the victim, I was half-relieved to find it wasn't Pasang or Gombu. Perhaps they were alive somewhere along the avalanche track. When I got to the victim's head, I was stunned to discover a man in a bush hat—one of Jackson Mallory's men! He also wore a down vest with the Foger Utility Group logo on it.

Even more dramatic was what I found on his feet.

The man wore something strapped onto the bottom of his hiking boots: huge, rubberized latex feet!

And they were facing backward.

And so Mallory's scheme was revealed to me.

Last night this man had started somewhere high on the Lhotse Face and run *downhill* wearing fake yeti feet. This way he could simulate the yeti's gargantuan stride. He wore the feet backward, of course, so that it looked like the creature was running uphill.

Very clever.

Since he was wearing the fake feet again, I figured the guy planned to lope down the glacier next. The idea was to keep us on a wild good chase. Meanwhile the Blue Wasp would do infrared scans of the mountain's high passes, a far more likely place to find a reclusive creature.

But of course he didn't count on getting caught in a killer avalanche.

Mallory's a slick fiend, I thought angrily. He got one person killed, and maybe my friends, too. As a cold blast of night air swirled off the slope, I realized that I'd better hurry back to camp, or else I'd end up yet another victim of Mallory's scheme. Darkness was swiftly blanketing the mountain.

I could see the warm multicolored glow of tents just a quarter mile down the valley. But as I staggered over the snow debris, I forgot that the Western Cwm is actually a moving glacier full of deep cracks. The avalanche, of course, had filled in a few crevasses. It had also rolled over a few thin snow bridges spanning crevasses, leaving them unbroken but highly unstable.

As I made a beeline toward Camp II, I threw caution to the wind. After just a few yards of struggle, I stepped on an innocent-looking mound of snow. *Crack!* And then I was falling.

I didn't fall far, and the landing into snow was soft enough. But when I looked up, I found myself stranded at the bottom of a steep ice trench, maybe ten to twelve feet deep. And this time I didn't have Gombu or a lucky ladder to help me out.

"Great," I said.

I wanted to beat on my head for being so reckless, but decided to conserve energy. *I'll beat on my head later*, I thought. The crevasse was narrow, and its walls were vertical, hard, and slick. Looking up, all I could see was a strip of clear, starry sky.

After a few desperate attempts, it was clear I had no way out.

"Help!" I yelled. "Hey! Bud! Help!"

The chances of my voice carrying clearly out of the trench and a quarter mile down the valley were slim, especially considering the ongoing flow of jet stream winds over Everest. Even at Base Camp you can hear the roar of wind from the higher reaches of the mountain.

On top of that, my throat was still raw and sore from the dryness, cold, and altitude.

"Okay," I said. "Okay. So I'm dead."

A wave a panic rolled over me. So I sat down and tried to calm my mind.

That's when I heard the warble. It was close by.

"Hey!" I called. "Hello? Who's there?"

I heard crunching footsteps up above. I jumped to my feet.

"Down here!" I squawked. "Hey! I'm down here!"

The crunching stopped. There was a moment of silence that seemed to go on for weeks. Then, suddenly, I saw the shadow of a large head and shoulders lean over the edge of the trench.

"Wow!" I said. "Dude! Hello! Boy, am I glad to see you, whoever you are! Can you get me out? Do you have a rope or something?"

I couldn't see the face, but in silhouette it looked like a large man wearing a furry Sherpa hat.

"Do you speak English, sir?" I asked, reaching my hand up toward him.

After a pause, the man reached down one of his arms. It was remarkably long.

I hopped up, trying to grab it. As I did, he seized my wrist in a powerful grip. Then he swung me out of the trench with ease.

I stood up to face him, saying, "Thanks! Thanks so much!" And then I froze.

By the snow-reflected moonlight I found myself face-to-face with a huge, shaggy hominid at least seven feet tall.

10

A Hairy Rescue

The creature in front of me was covered with coarse dark fur. Its long arms stretched almost to its knees. As it turned toward the moonlight, I could see it had a conical skull with a protruding jaw. Human-looking eyes examined me with obvious curiosity.

I probably should have been terrified. But I wasn't, not after the initial shock.

Something told me that this yeti was young—a teenager too maybe. Still young and impulsive enough to be curious about the strangers on the mountain, and not knowing enough yet to stay safely hidden like the rest of his people.

"Hey," I said, shivering. "'Sup, dude?"

He tilted his head a bit sideways.

I pointed at myself, then turned and pointed toward the glowing tents of Camp II. "I need to go there," I said. I repeated this sign language a couple more times. "If *I* . . . don't go *there* soon . . . I'm going to *freeze* to death." I wrapped my arms around my torso and shivered. "I'm cold. *Brrrrrrr!*"

The yeti looked from me to the distant camp, following my gestures. When I shivered, he grunted. Then he turned and moved across the snow. For such a big guy, he moved with amazing agility.

"Where you going?" I called.

He stopped and turned to me, waiting.

"Should I follow you?" I asked. As I said this I pointed at myself, then at him.

The creature made an odd throaty sound, almost like the chirp of a bird, but deeper.

"I'll take that as a yes," I said. "And by the way, I'm officially naming you Harry."

When I started following him, he turned and continued across the snow. He glanced back to check on me several times as he led me directly across the glacial valley toward the southwest face of Everest, moving perpendicular to where the camp was located. For a second I thought maybe he didn't understand my request, or maybe he was deliberately leading me somewhere else—to his man-eating tribe, perhaps. *Look mom, dinner followed me home!* But these crazy thoughts evaporated as he veered back toward Camp II again.

In fact for the next thirty minutes we zigzagged back and forth around visible and not-so-visible crevasses until we ended up just a hundred feet or so from the tents. Then he stopped, clearly reluctant to go farther.

"That's cool," I assured him, holding up my hands in the universal gesture for stop. "You stay here."

The yeti crouched into a squatting position and stared uneasily at the camp.

"It's okay, Harry," I said.

I turned and took a few steps toward the camp. When I looked back, the yeti was gliding gracefully around a low snow drift toward the Everest face. He was moving toward one of our motion detector setups. I stopped and watched him.

A few seconds later I heard the electronic beep of a thermal detector. Several flashbulbs went off, and I heard the creature grunt and warble. My face was ice cold, but I managed a smile: *I got my yeti photo,* I thought.

But then I heard a loud clang and a horrifying howl

of pain. Then a piercing alarm split the cold night. As I turned toward these sounds, I saw flashing white lights. I started running to them. When I got there, the yeti was snarling and sitting on the ground, tugging violently on a bear trap that had snapped shut on his leg. An attached module was emitting the light and the earsplitting alarm.

I heard shouting from the camp, and looked over to see Bud and several Sherpas bounding over the snow with flashlights bobbing. When the lights trained on the huge howling creature, they stopped. The Sherpas spoke excitedly in their language; I could make out references to *dzu-teh, dzu-teh!*

"Bud!" I yelled. "Help me get this freaking trap off his leg!"

"Are you kidding me?" cried Bud.

"We gotta help him!" I shouted.

But before we could make another move, the rhythmic chop of helicopter rotors grew louder, and a blinding white spotlight suddenly burst from the sky, illuminating the whole scene.

You guessed it: The Blue Wasp had arrived.

"What's going on?" shouted Bud.

"Mallory piggybacked on our detectors!" I yelled

back. Now I knew why he was hovering over us all day; he must have marked their locations, then snuck in his traps in the night.

The copter dropped quickly, and before we knew it a squad of armed men in bush hats surrounded the howling, frightened yeti. One fired a volley of tranquilizer darts; two others rushed in with a large net and tossed it. I felt terrible for this creature who had just saved my life. The bush-hatters seized the net and hauled the poor thrashing hominid toward the helicopter. Its struggles got weaker as the tranquilizer took effect. Then the Blue Wasp rose vertically into the night sky. As it banked to the southwest, its spotlight snapped off, leaving darkness and silence in its wake.

The whole operation had lasted less then sixty seconds.

"Did that just happen?" mumbled Bud. "Did I just see what I think I saw?"

I nodded numbly. "Yes," I said.

Suddenly my legs started trembling.

Bud took my arm. "Dude, you okay?" he asked.

"Dude, I need a warm sleeping bag," I said.

"Get you to tent," said one of the Sherpas, a

younger fellow named Dawa who was a particularly good card player.

They helped me stumble to our tent, which was basking in the glow of the catalytic heater. I'd never felt such glorious warmth.

"Where's Pasang?" asked Bud. "And Gombu? Did the tracks lead you to that big beast?"

I put my head down. "I don't know where they are," I said.

And then I told them the whole story.

"Oh my gosh," was all Bud could say.

My eyelids felt heavier than they'd ever felt in my life.

The next morning, our fourth in Nepal, I woke to the sound of music. Okay, it wasn't actual music; rather it was two voices that *sounded* like music to me, right outside our tent.

"Tom Swift, are you in there?" called the first voice.

"Pasang!" I yelled groggily.

The tent flap unzipped and Pasang burst in and gave me a big hug.

"You're alive!" we both said at the same time. Then we both laughed.

"I'm ready for your game of cards," called the other voice. Of course it was Gombu.

I was already fully dressed; I'd been so exhausted the night before that Bud had just basically stuffed me into my bag after pulling off my boots. So Pasang and I crawled right outside my tent, where Gombu stood with some other Sherpas and Bud, who'd been up for two hours already.

Gombu embraced me, then said, "We saw you go down and hoped you know how to ride."

"You didn't go down too?" I asked him.

"No!"

Pasang said, "Tom, it was a loose snow avalanche, with no hard slabs. And the point release was just above us, so the track was still narrow when it hit us. Father was up higher, so he just dug in and rode it out. He's strong, you know."

"Yeah," I said, grinning. "I know."

Gombu had his arm locked around my waist. It felt like he could snap me in half if he wanted.

"I just hold the rope," he said. "My daughter is very smart, you know."

"Yes, I think you mentioned that before, sirdar," I said with a laugh.

"When I looked up, I could see that it was loose snow, like I said, not a slab avalanche," said Pasang. "So I knew we had a chance. I started kicking and scooting, trying to get on its outside edge. Father was dug in, but he swung the rope to help me." Her eyes sparkled as she looked at me. "I got wide enough to miss the main force of the slide. But then I saw you go down."

"Yeah," I said. "I went down, all right—*way* down."

Bud shook his head. "Dude, I can't believe you swam halfway down the Lhotse Face. That has to be a first in Everest climbing history."

"Weren't you scared?" asked Pasang.

"I didn't have enough time to be scared," I said. "Seriously, it happened so fast, I just reacted on pure instinct. I was at the bottom and half buried before I could think."

Pasang's eyes darkened. "We didn't trigger it," she said. "Like I said, it was a loose snow avalanche. That type is triggered at a single spot called the point release. The snow fans outward below that point, collecting as it spreads downhill."

"So you're saying something—or someone— above us triggered this release," I said.

"Possibly," said Pasang.

"Wow," I said. "You don't think . . . ?" I didn't finish the question. I looked over at Bud. He glared back at me.

"Jackson Mallory is a creeping slime mold," he said.

I nodded. "Yes," I said. "There's that."

Pasang turned to me. "We heard about your visitor."

"He wasn't a visitor," I said. "*I* was the visitor. He *lives* here."

Pasang nodded in agreement. "And he saved your life," she said.

"Yes," I said. "And now I owe him one."

Bud gave me an excited look. "Your eyes are glowing like hot coals, dude," he said. "I've been your friend long enough to know what that means."

"What does it mean?" asked Pasang.

"It means yeti liberation," I said.

Everyone got excited about this. Nobody wanted Jackson Mallory to drag the yeti back as some sort of hunting prize. The Sherpas who'd seen how Mallory had treated the creature—a native of these mountains, like them—were disgusted and angry.

So everybody was on board with Operation Harry Rescue.

Unfortunately nobody knew where he was at the moment. The other Sherpas reported that Mallory's team had abandoned Base Camp the day before and flew off in their helicopter to some undisclosed location.

"Great," said Bud. "Now what?"

Gombu smiled. He gestured to his team of guides.

"We find him," he said.

As we put our heads together to formulate a rescue plan, Bud tried to get onto the Internet for some quick research. But all he could get was a blank screen. We quickly discovered that someone has sabotaged the GeoDome.

"Wow, it's sneakily but totally trashed," I said, examining the damage.

"Mallory's thugs must have done it," said Bud grimly. "He didn't want us to break the news about the yeti discovery first."

Then I suddenly remembered: "The camera!" I said.

We rushed out to the detector/camera array that the yeti had tripped the night before. Sure enough, it was gone.

"Unbelievable," I said. "They must have nabbed it during all the commotion."

Bud shook his head. "Now we don't even have pictures to prove we saw him first," he said.

"Then we'll just have to make sure Mallory has nothing to show either," I said.

Part of me saw this as a straight-up competition against Jackson Mallory and his cruel, brutal methods. But I couldn't shake the vision of the yeti's eyes: first their bright curiosity as he'd helped me out of the ice trench, and second their panic and pain and fear as he thrashed in the snow, leg locked in a trap, tranquilizer darts jutting from his back. The more I thought about it, the more I didn't care if anybody knew I'd seen the yeti first. In fact I began to think it would be best if *nobody* knew. I knew that wasn't possible anymore, but I felt bad for the snowman and his abominable treatment at the hands of Jackson Mallory and other men.

Later that afternoon, we got our first break. Two

guides from Gombu's team returned with the location of Mallory's new camp.

Pasang translated for us. "They say he's out on the Kangshung Glacier, east of Everest." She pulled out a relief map of the area and pointed to Mallory's campsite location. "It's remote here, but fairly flat and long."

"Perfect," I said. "Can we land down here?" I pointed to a spot farther down the glacier. "I want to approach from below."

"Yes," she said. "That bowl is very flat." She pointed at a jagged ridgeline on the map. "And this low ridge will cut off their view of our approach. It rises maybe fifty feet and overlooks the cirque where they're camped," she said. "It's very rocky. Many places to hide." She grinned. "It should be fun."

I grinned back. "Then let's load up the Sub-Orbiter," I said.

After packing what we needed into the cargo hold, I plotted a roundabout flight path so we could drop onto the Kangshung Glacier without being spotted by Mallory and his crew. Then Bud, Pasang, Gombu, and I boarded the aircraft and I flew us to our destination.

◇ ◇ ◇

Three hours later it was dusk and seventeen below zero outside. A wind gust rocked the Sub-Orbiter, where we all sat, waiting.

"Gee, what a lovely night," said Bud, looking out the copilot's window at the bleak dark beauty of the glacier.

"Perfect weather," I said.

"For what?" asked Pasang, who sat in a passenger seat behind me.

"For stealth, of course," I said. "Okay, let's gear up." I stood and gestured to my pilot's seat. "Bud?" I said.

"Roger that," he replied, and hopped into my seat. He punched a button on the console and added, "Let's do a final com-link check."

"Okay," I said. I pulled on my polar hat and adjusted its earflaps. "This is Tango Sierra. Do you read me? Over."

My voice came out of the console speaker at the same moment I spoke. Bud grinned and said, "Hotel here. I read you loud and clear. Over."

A voice-activated radio headset was wired into my hat. Its mouthpiece, a slim wire with a mike at the end, curved forward on the inside of the earflap, hidden from anyone looking at me.

"Test looks good," I said.

"Roger," said Bud. "Over and out."

Bud was going to monitor the operation from our headquarters ("Hotel") here in the Sub-Orbiter while Pasang, Gombu, and I executed the field plan. The three of us slipped on night-vision goggles, and I grabbed a handful of red waypoint markers— tiny transmitters that emitted an electronic signal. Then we exited the cozy warmth of the cabin. With Gombu in the lead, as usual, we began our trek up the windswept Kangshung valley toward Mallory's camp location.

Gombu guided us around several horizontal crevasses and ice walls. Each time we changed direction, I dropped a waypoint marker. We zigzagged across the glacier nearly a half mile until finally reaching the boulder-strewn slope of our destination, the low ridge. The night was bitter cold.

"Ah, there they are," I said.

"Like sitting ducks," said Pasang.

I could sense the excitement in her voice. She was enjoying this adventure.

From the ridgetop we could see the glowing tents of Mallory's camp below. It was about a hundred yards away. Their helicopter, the Blue Wasp, sat nearby. As the map had shown, the ridge curled in a fishhook around the left side of the camp.

"Okay, here's where we split up," I said. I whacked Pasang on the arm. "Good luck, pal."

She smiled. "Right," she said. "Have fun."

"Oh, I will," I said.

Gombu and Pasang moved off to the left, following the ridgetop toward the campsite. Meanwhile I zoomed my night-vision scope on the camp and spotted the yeti. He was cruelly chained and left outside, sitting against a mobile generator post. I could see that he held the leg that had been in the bear trap, cradling it with both arms. I took a deep breath to control my anger, then I started down the ridge.

As I got closer, I heard a mournful howl from the ridge above. I ducked behind a boulder as one of the bush-hat men popped out of a tent.

"Did you hear that?" he called across the camp.

More howls wafted down from the ridge, carried and distorted by gusts of frigid wind. Other men emerged from tents. Jackson Mallory himself stepped out, wielding a hunting rifle. *Splat!* Something hit his tent, splattering white. The men started ducking. Now projectiles were flying into the camp.

Snowballs!

One of them nailed Mallory, sending his blue bush hat flying.

"Oooh, nice shot, Pasang!" I murmured to myself.

"Are those *yetis* up there?" called one man to Mallory.

"Take them out!" howled Mallory in his bass growl.

Normally I would have been worried after hearing that, but I almost laughed as I pictured a bunch of clowns in bush hats trying to catch up to Pasang and Gombu, two of the best Sherpas in Nepal. Half of these men would end up at the bottom of ice chasms, I figured.

Mallory jammed his bush hat back on his head.

"Let's get the bird fired up!" he roared.

He and two of his men headed off toward the Blue Wasp while the rest fumbled to pull on boots and parkas, then stumbled off into the darkness in search of yeti snowball tossers.

Amazingly the entire crew vacated the camp. Within seconds the place was entirely deserted.

I shook my head. "What a bunch of losers," I said.

I moved quickly and approached the chained yeti. He snarled angrily at me and rose into a coiled crouch. I pulled back my parka hood and pushed the night vision goggles up onto my forehead.

"Hey, dude, it's me," I said. I held up my hands in the universal sign that says, *I come in peace and unarmed.* "See? It's okay."

I could see in his eyes that he still didn't trust me completely, and I didn't blame him. But I had to move fast, so I dug in my pocket and pulled out one of my favorite little inventions: a mini laser cutter. It was no bigger than a small flashlight, but could emit controlled laser pulses with output up to one full kilowatt per burst. It could cut through chain links in seconds.

Nearby I heard the Blue Wasp rotors whine and begin to churn.

"Easy, fella," I said calmly, in the most soothing tone I could muster. "Easy, man."

I reached out my free hand slowly. The yeti

watched it warily, but he didn't recoil or lash out when I finally grabbed the chain. Then I went right to work. I gently took his wrists and then carefully sliced through the metal cuffs that the chains were attached to. Next I sliced the cuffs on his ankles.

"Is your leg okay?" I asked, pointing at his leg then rubbing my own to mime what I meant.

He gave a moan; a bear trap can snap both bones in a normal man's leg. But I guessed that a yeti leg was much sturdier, and I was right. Still crouching, he wrapped both of his hairy hands around what I'm sure was an aching shin, moaned loudly again, but then stood up.

"Can you walk?" I said. I backed up and motioned with my hands for him to follow me, saying, "Come on! Let's get out of here, bro."

He staggered for a second, limping. But then, moving with agility once again stunning for a creature so big, he darted off into the night. In mere seconds he was gone, well out of my sight radius.

"Okay, Hotel, the mark is away. Over," I said into my earflap.

"Roger that, Tango Sierra," said Bud in my ear. "Now get out of there."

As I reached up to pull my night-vision goggles down over my eyes, a deep voice boomed behind me: "A poacher in my camp? Well, well, well."

I spun around.

Jackson Mallory walked around a tent. He lowered his hunting rifle until it pointed at my chest.

"What are you doing here, boy?" he rumbled.

And then he noticed that his prize game was gone.

His bellow of rage rose high over the Himalayas.

11

Kite vs. Sled

As you know, I've always been fascinated by how mechanical things work.

I'm sure that's true of anyone who considers himself an inventor. For example, the summer when I was ten, I got obsessed with how locks work. I spent weeks learning everything about them.

So as I sat there in the subzero Himalayan night, chained like a beast to the mobile generator post, I knew exactly what I needed to do to unlock the cuffs clamped on my legs. Unfortunately I didn't have the tools I needed. But I knew where to get them.

"Good night, Mr. Swift," said Jackson Mallory as he stood over me. "I know it's cold. But your winter outfit looks adequate." He laughed harshly. "I expect you'll lose only your toes and maybe a finger or two to frostbite by morning."

"Thanks, Mr. Mallory," I said. "Sleep warm."

"Oh, I will," he said. He reached in his pocket and pulled out my mini laser cutter. "I'm really glad we searched you so thoroughly. I wouldn't want you out wandering the glacier at night. It's dangerous, you know."

His mocking tone was really getting on my nerves.

"Yes," I said. "I understand there are yetis roaming *free* out there."

This hardened Mallory's face a bit. "You shouldn't have meddled in my business," he said with undisguised menace.

"Sorry," I said.

"Yes, well, we have plenty of yeti evidence gathered," he said, indicating a small black storage container next to his tent. "Photos, bioscans, hair and other DNA samples. And, Swift, when you look down at the toeless stubs of your feet in the future, you can remember *my* success and *your* failure."

Several of his men, now clad in polar gear, tromped into the camp. No surprise—they'd had no luck finding the snowball raiders on the ridge. But now they were setting up small, dishlike devices around the perimeter of the camp.

"What are they doing?" I asked.

Mallory watched the activity.

"Setting up infrared detectors," he said with casual menace. "I'm sure you're familiar with these devices. Anything warm that gets within fifty yards of this camp—anything with a human heat signature—will set off alarms." He turned and gave me a nasty look. "If that happens, the intruder will be shot on sight."

"So, no human or mammal or, like, anything *warm* can approach the camp without getting shot?" I repeated.

Mallory looked at me. "Yes," he said. "That's what I said."

"Okay," I said.

Mallory bent down to enter his tent vestibule. "We'll release you in the morning," he said.

"Excellent!" I said.

He turned and looked at me. "You're a strange kid," he said.

I nodded. In my ear, I heard Bud's voice say, "Ready for instructions here. Over."

"Just chill a minute," I whispered.

"Like you right now?" After a pause he added, "Okay, maybe that wasn't funny."

After Mallory and his crew doused their tent lanterns one by one, I spoke low. "So did you hear? Stay away from the camp, dude. You'll get shot if you approach. Are Pasang and Gombu back?"

"Yep, they're here," replied Bud.

"Okay, good," I murmured. "Then listen up."

Bud listened to my instructions, reviewed them with me once, and then signed off.

"Preparing to deploy cavalry now," he said. "I'll be in touch."

"Roger that," I said. "Out."

My arms were totally free, but the shackles on my legs were heavy-duty leg irons. I examined the locks once again, noting their standard pin tumbler design, which made me very, very happy. If they'd been high-security cylinder locks, I'd have a much more difficult time.

Then I sat back to wait.

I stomped my feet every few seconds, trying to keep blood flowing. Mallory was right; even with my space-age boots, a full night exposed to the wicked Himalayan cold would not be good for my toes. Of course I didn't plan to spend a full night here.

It took about thirty minutes, but the cavalry finally arrived.

The wind was swirling and kicking up dustings of dry snow, and that distant Everest jet stream roar filled the silences in between, so I wasn't sure I heard the footsteps at first.

But then I saw him—good old A.N.G., his jointed hydraulic legs stepping lightly across the snowpack. He'd been following the waypoint markers I'd dropped, of course, to avoid falling in a crevasse.

I had A.N.G.'s remote control tucked safely into a secret pocket of my parka. I quickly pulled it out and tapped it with the silver-alloy fingertip of my glove; A.N.G. halted. Then I guided him very slowly and silently through the tents of the campsite.

A.N.G. is not an animal, so he hadn't set off the infrared detectors. Genius, huh?

When he finally reached me, I opened a small compartment on his snout. There, as instructed, Bud had stashed my lock-pick snap gun and a set of picking needles. To use it, I'd have to use bare hands, but I didn't expect it would take long, so the exposure would be minimal. But just to be safe, I nabbed a small pack of exothermic chemical hand warmers—another item Bud had packed into A.N.G.'s snout compartment for me—and popped one open.

Then I got to work. It took just minutes to pick open both of the leg shackles.

"How's it going?" called Bud in my ear.

"I'm free," I said quietly. "I'm making the goods switch now."

First I stood and silently unloaded the light gear strapped on A.N.G.'s back. Then, moving very slowly to avoid crunching footsteps, I walked toward Mallory's tent and nabbed the black storage container full of his yeti evidence. I strapped this onto A.N.G.'s back.

Finally I waited for gusts of wind. With each gust, I walked A.N.G. a couple of steps farther out of the campsite heading down the glacier. When he got far enough away, I punched in a special retrack code that would send A.N.G. retracing his exact route from waypoint to waypoint back to the Sub-Orbiter. The last I saw him, A.N.G. was climbing the low ridge behind the campsite.

Then I carefully donned the gear I'd unloaded. Yep, you guessed it: my Swift-Foil kite and my ultralight snowboard. I secured the kite harness and adjusted the horizontal computer-control bar. The kite itself was still folded up and strapped tight so the wind wouldn't push me around.

Then I sat down to wait again.

Time seemed to whirl endlessly, like wind in the mountain passes.

Why was I waiting, you ask?

Well, remember the infrared detectors surrounding the camp? The instant I tried to make a break, the detectors would go off. Mallory and his armed thugs would be hot on my tail. I wanted to give A.N.G. enough time to deliver his cargo to Bud before I made my midnight run down the glacier.

After almost forty minutes I started to worry. What if A.N.G. was lost? What if he fell into a crevasse? What if Yo's bug fix didn't work and he was dancing in a circle somewhere slippery right now? *Maybe I shouldn't be waiting like this,* I thought. *Maybe I should just make my break now.*

I kept checking in with Bud, but he had nothing to report . . . until finally, a few minutes later, he said, "Wait. Wait, I see something." After a pause, he added, "Yes! That's A.N.G.! He's back, dude! Pasang, Gombu, I've deactivated him, go ahead and load him in the cargo hold. And, you, Tango Sierra . . . get out of that campsite, now!"

"Roger that," I said. "Hit that ignition button I showed you, Hotel. I'll be right home."

"Igniting engines now," said Bud. "Good luck, man. Over and out."

Carrying my snowboard, I walked quickly across the campsite.

And an alarm went off.

"Oh come on!" I said. I hadn't expected an alarm so soon; I hadn't even reached the last pair of tents yet. But somehow one of the thermal detectors picked up my heat signature and started wailing like a banshee.

I dropped my board, kicked my feet into the bindings, and reached down to tighten them. The downhill grade was very shallow here, so I started out slow.

"He's gone!" shouted a man somewhere behind me.

Then I heard Mallory's deep voice as it boomed, "Where's the Swift boy?"

"There!" hollered someone else. "There he is!"

Up ahead, the low ridge loomed in the moonlight. The sky was crystal clear now, and the moon's reflection on the white snow made it seem more like dawn than the dead of night. The ground would slope uphill soon, I could see, so I reached back to pull the kite-straps loose and unfurl the sail.

Immediately I took off.

Wow! The gusts swooping down off of Everest caught the kite and hurled me forward. I banked around the last tents just as men crawled out of them. Then I pulled back on the control bar as I reached the rocky ridge. Up I went!

Behind me I heard a motor chug to life, then another. I chanced a backward glance and caught sight of two low rounded shapes rocketing across the snow toward me with a loud rasping engine whine.

"Snowmobiles!" I exclaimed. "Bud, they're following me on snowmobiles!"

"Uh-oh," said Bud. There was a pause. Then he added, "Tom, I'm putting Pasang on."

I caught a stiff updraft as I carved around a boulder on the upslope of the ridge. I flew high over the ridgetop and hung motionless for an exhilarating few seconds. Then I banked around in a quick circle to see my pursuers. Sure enough, two droning snowmobiles with bright halogen headlamps bounced up the ridge behind me.

"Tom, do you hear me?" Now Pasang's voice was in my ear.

"Yeah, I hear you," I said.

"I'm going to guide you back," she said.

"I *know* the way back," I replied.

"But I know a better way," she said quickly. "A way that I guarantee Jackson Mallory doesn't know."

I felt a quick pop of tension, then release, in the control bar, and immediately heard the sound of a gunshot. Then I heard a whistling and looked up to see a small hole in the kite sail. Mallory was a big game hunter, and probably a pretty crack shot. The bullet had hit the kite before the sound of the rifle report reached me.

I quickly banked down the far side of the ridge to cut off his shooting angle.

"He's shooting at me!" I exclaimed.

Pasang's voice grew terser. "Tom, have you cleared the ridge yet?"

"Yes," I said. I dropped to the ground and started

carving down a flat downhill stretch of the Kangshung glacier.

"Okay," directed Pasang. "Veer left toward the ice cliff."

"Okay," I replied.

I carved hard to the left. I could see the eastern face of Everest rising above me. Ahead was an ice wall shining in the moonlight. Behind I could hear the roar of the snowmobiles as they crested over the ridge. Then I heard another gunshot. I didn't feel any jolt in my rigging, so the shot must have missed.

"Stick very close to the ice wall as you head down the glacier valley," said Pasang.

I heard a shout and a tumbling, crunching sound. Glancing back, I saw one of the snowmobiles wipe out, its headlight spinning wildly.

"One down, one to go," I cried.

Another gust of wind pushed me faster. I bounced over mogul after mogul, occasionally peeking back to see the remaining snowmobile bouncing behind me. It was very fast and closing the gap. It was a two-man sled; I could see the passenger braced and leveling a hunting rifle at my kite again.

"Swift!" bellowed the unmistakable voice of

Jackson Mallory. "Swift! You're going *down!*"

Again my kite shuddered from the hit before I heard the report of the rifle. This shot tore an even bigger hole in the sail. Now I was struggling; the control wasn't as smooth.

"He hit my kite again," I reported, voice shaking as my board bounced again and again on the surface. "I'm losing some control."

Pasang spoke quickly now. "Do you see a big snow mound rising in front of you yet?"

I could see one just down the slope. "Yes!" I said. "A big one!"

"Head straight for it," said Pasang. "And get ready to lift."

I heard another gunshot, another miss. My kite was a pretty big target, but I knew Mallory was bouncing hard on the snowmobile. I followed Pasang's instructions and started rising up the massive, rounded snow mound. I could hear the sled closing in behind me; the driver was really hauling, and the engine sounded deep and powerful. Soon Mallory would have a shot he couldn't possibly miss, he was so close.

"Stay on the ground over the top of the mound,"

said Pasang. "But be ready to lift! You'll pass over a hidden crevasse, a big one. If it collapses . . ."

She didn't have to finish the sentence. I saw the plan now.

I turned the control bar to lower the kite as far as possible, pulling me straight ahead across the snow. I put all of my weight into the bouncing board. Behind me the roar of the sled was louder. I could almost feel Mallory's targeting sight on my back.

Then the world below me gave way.

With a quick twist of the control bar I kicked the kite upward, and I followed with a pretty strong jolt of the harness. For a second I thought I was losing control, but then I rose gracefully.

"Jump it!" shrieked Mallory to his driver behind me. "Jump it!"

I glanced over my shoulder just as the snowmobile leaped off the edge of the crevasse. It was a noble, even glorious attempt.

But he didn't make it.

I had no idea how deep the crevasse was. I didn't know if he survived. Mallory is still falling today, for all I know. But I kept going. When I touched down lightly on the other side, I could see the blue white xenon taxi lights of my Sub-Orbiter just below me. I glided down the last slope.

"Here he comes!" cried Pasang in my ear.

As I carved to a stop next to the aircraft, the others scrambled out of the hatch. I quickly twisted my kite to the ground and unhitched the harness. Without speaking we folded everything up and stashed it in the cargo hold next to A.N.G. and the storage container. Then we hustled aboard.

I took the controls and lifted us toward the starry pinpoints that canopied the Kangshung valley.

12

On Top of the World

Packing up camp the next afternoon was a bittersweet experience. The weather was beautiful; the lines of Everest were etched clearly against a bright blue sky. After we finished sliding our gear into the Sub-Orbiter's cargo hold, several of the Sherpas gathered around and we played Slapjack for a couple of wild, laughing hours.

We had already said good-bye to Pasang and Gombu very early that morning. In fact when Pasang woke us, it was still dark. I fired up the lantern and let her into our tent.

Bud sat up in his sleeping bag, looking like a large mutant caterpillar.

"I don't recall sleeping," he grumbled.

Pasang laughed. "We have to go," she said. "The

Australians got a good weather report, and they want to make a summit try over the next three days."

She looked at me.

I suddenly felt a wave of stupidity wash over me. I tried to think of something to say, but nothing came to mind.

"Uh, well, you know, don't fall or anything," I said.

Pasang nodded. She looked a little funny too. "Do you have my e-mail address?" she said.

"Yes," I said. "I sent a note to my dad about good aerospace programs. He's looking into it."

"Okay," she said.

I nodded. "Okay, well," I said.

We hugged kind of awkwardly. Then she turned to Bud with a grin and wrapped her arms around the big caterpillar.

"It was good meeting you, Bud Barclay," she said.

"I want you to know something," said Bud.

Pasang pulled back and held him at arm's length. "What?" she asked with an amused glint in her eyes.

Bud took a deep breath. Then he said, "I never cheated at cards."

"Not once?" she asked.

"Never."

Pasang nodded. She said, "I don't believe you."

Bud grinned.

Outside, we heard Gombu's voice. "Tom Swift!" he called. "Come climb to the top with us!"

I started laughing. Gombu had become one of my favorite people ever. I stuck my head out of the tent flap.

"Maybe next time," I said. "See, I have a few ideas for things that might make life easier in these nutty mountains."

Gombu laughed heartily. "You come back sometime," he said. "Bring more robots! We take you to the top of the world!"

Pasang crawled out past me and then stood by her father. As they both looked at me, I realized that nothing could ever replace these people. Least of all a silly robot.

"I'll be in touch," I said to Pasang. "I promise."

"Good," she said. "I'm a good writer."

"Very smart girl," said Gombu, beaming at his daughter. "Very smart. Did I tell you that?"

They both laughed, then they waved good-bye and trudged uphill to the Australian campsite, a busy place. I could feel the electric charge in the air. An Everest summit attempt! Really, what could be more exciting and nerve wracking?

The answer: nothing I could think of.

As the Sub-Orbiter rose, I swung the nose to face up the Khumbu Glacier. I had Q.U.I.P. back up and running, and we went through our final flight checklist. The autopilot was ready to engage. Our return flight would be a bit longer, with a refueling stop planned in southern Spain; but we'd still be home in just three hours.

Bud stared out at the icefall. "Well, dude, your Everest gig was a major success, I'd say," he said.

"Yeah, A.N.G. came through like a champ," I said. "My snow-kiting went well too."

"And you found a yeti," said Bud.

I looked over at him. "Did I?"

Bud grinned at me.

Sure, I had the goods to prove my story—if I wanted to. But something told me that revealing the truth would just attract more heartless hunters like Jackson Mallory. It would be bad for the yeti, bad for the Sherpa, and just plain bad for the great mountain.

"Man, the scoop of the century dropped right in my lap," said Bud, shaking his head. "Too bad."

"What's too bad?" I asked.

"Too bad you can't recall anything and have no comment on the matter, not even off the record," he said.

"Oh, that," I said with a chuckle. "Yes, it *is* too bad."

I glided up the glacier, over the white bowl of the Western Cwm, and then lifted vertically up the blue ice of the Lhotse Face. The avalanche track was still easy to see, and then I spotted a team of climbers snaking up the face. One wore a bright blue parka. The team halted and turned to gaze up at us. Then they waved.

I waggled my wings.

I banked left and took one last loop around the top of the world.

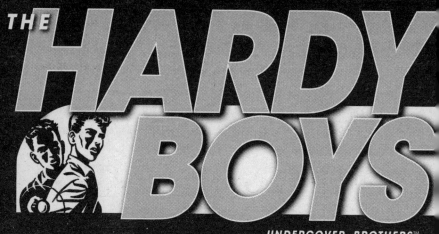

PENDRAGON

Bobby Pendragon is a seemingly normal fourteen-year-old boy. He has a family, a home, and a possible new girlfriend. But something happens to Bobby that changes his life forever.

HE IS CHOSEN TO DETERMINE
THE COURSE OF HUMAN EXISTENCE.

Pulled away from the comfort of his family and suburban home, Bobby is launched into the middle of an immense, interdimensional conflict involving racial tensions, threatened ecosystems, and more. It's a journey of danger and discovery for Bobby, and his success or failure will do nothing less than determine the fate of the world. . . .

PENDRAGON

by D. J. MacHale

Book One: The Merchant of Death
Book Two: The Lost City of Faar
Book Three: The Never War
Book Four: The Reality Bug
Book Five: Black Water

Coming Soon: Book Six: The Rivers of Zadaa

From Aladdin Paperbacks • Published by Simon & Schuster

Ever wonder what happened after **Jack** came down the beanstalk?

Or what became of **Hansel and Gretel?**

Read all of P. W. Catanese's Further Tales to find out. . . .
But beware: These are NOT your parents' fairy tales.

And coming soon . . . "Mirror, Mirror on the Wall,
NOW who's the fairest of them all?" *The Mirror's Tale*
by P. W. Catanese